Cheryl,
Best case of mistaken
identity.
♡ Rochelle
Paige

IDENTITY CRISIS

Rochelle Paige

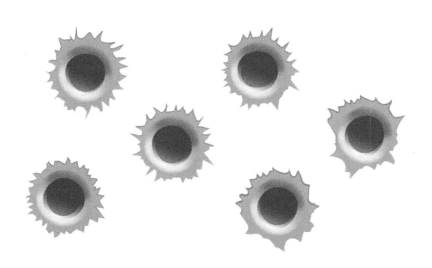

COPYRIGHT

DEDICATION

Elle

*A true friend supports you because
they want to see you succeed.*

Thank you for being a true friend. Identity Crisis
would not be what it is without all your help.

A Note From The Author

I've always been fascinated by stories about the men and women who bravely serve our country, especially those in special operations units. Their uncommon desire to succeed and unflinching commitment to accomplish their mission leave me awe-struck. Writing a book featuring a character who is a Navy SEAL has been a privilege. As such, I feel it necessary to point out that some liberties have been taken with SEAL training and mission operation to fit the needs of this story.

CHAPTER 1

Blaine

Sweeping my gaze across the glitzy casino, I absently ran my finger under the collar of my shirt. Damn bow tie felt like it was strangling me. I couldn't help but wonder how the hell I'd managed to find myself here, living in the lap of luxury with such a cushy job. Even though this had been my life for the past year, it was so far removed from my childhood, I felt like I would never belong. When my phone buzzed, I yanked it out of my pocket — relieved by the distraction and hoping like hell it would help me pull my head out of my ass.

When I glanced down at the notification, I was surprised to see a text from Serena Taylor. Talk about a blast from the past. The last time I saw her was before my first deployment overseas. We'd met for dinner at my hotel when I went to Atlanta to see her and I'd be lying if I said I hadn't been hoping for more than just dinner. Training and the pre-deployment workup that followed were grueling and the idea of hooking back up with the girl next door, one who'd fueled most of my high school fantasies, was more appealing than hitting a bar and picking up some random chick wanting to bang a SEAL. It didn't take long for me to feel like I'd been there and done that.

I was surprised when things didn't work out as planned. We had a nice dinner and Serena caught me up on all the news from back home, but the spark wasn't there anymore. She wasn't the same girl I'd known growing up, and it wasn't just the move to a big city far from home. Gone was the girl who had been soft and vulnerable, in her place was a sleek and sophisticated stranger. I'd been looking for a piece of home to hold onto while I was overseas and it didn't take long to realize Serena wasn't it.

I wasn't an idiot, though. I still would have banged her, except, it turned out, she had a boyfriend. When she talked about the new man in her life, the reason for the change became immediately clear. She'd hooked up with some rich guy who wanted her as his arm candy. I was disappointed to realize the girl I'd cared for had turned into a woman who wanted nice things more than she wanted a good man in her life.

But it didn't stop me from worrying about her. She was still the girl I grew up with, the first one I'd ever kissed. Hell, she let me pop her cherry when we were sophomores.

Before she left, I made sure she had my contact information and I told her she better use it if she ever needed anything. Time had passed and I hadn't heard from her again—until now.

Serena: I'm in trouble. Need help.
Me: What kind of trouble?

Serena: The kind where I'm on the run and looking for a place to hide out.

Me: Still in Atlanta?

Serena: Yes

The only time I'd ever been there was my quick trip to see her, so I didn't have any contacts available to help with something like this. But I knew someone who could find some quickly.

Me: Hold on.

With the nine-hour time difference, odds were high Brody was sound asleep. He'd become a night owl ever since we made it home. I pulled up his name in my contacts and listened as the call rolled to voicemail, redialing two more times before he finally picked up.

"You better be calling me to bail your asses out of jail," he rasped in a low tone.

"Like your brother wouldn't be able to get his hands on as much cash as we needed at the drop of a hat," I reminded him.

His snort of laughter made it clear he was just yanking my chain. "Then why the fuck are you calling me this early in the morning?"

"Do you know anyone in Atlanta who can help someone lay low for a couple days?"

"Someone?"

"Serena," I sighed, knowing an interrogation would soon follow. Not only did Brody know me better than any other person alive, including my past with Serena, he was the reason my life had changed so much in the last year.

As someone who saw their mom poorly treated by wealthy people, I used to despise them. My father died when I was five, leaving her to raise me on her own. They'd been high school sweethearts and married young. With no education or job experience, she ended up cleaning houses to make a living.

She was damn good at her job, but that didn't mean the families who hired her ever saw her as a real person. In their eyes, she was a convenience—a disposable one, at that. If something was broken, blame the maid. Can't find a piece of jewelry? Blame the maid. It didn't matter whether she had done anything wrong, or that it was usually their spoiled kid at fault. The bottom line was: she was replaceable and her wealthy employers never had a problem letting her go. Watching her accept their mistreatment, year after year, left me with a chip on my shoulder the size of a boulder.

Needless to say, I wanted better for my mom, and myself. My grades in high school were good, but not great since I'd juggled school, sports, and a part-time job to help lessen the load. With a full ride scholarship out of the question, college wasn't an option for me. I finally found my way out when I joined the Navy. It broke my mom's heart when I enlisted. She was scared to death of losing me too, but she accepted it like she did everything else in her life: with grace. I comforted myself with the knowledge that I didn't need much to maintain my bachelor lifestyle and would be able to send money to her every month.

If I was going to dedicate my life to the military, I was determined to be the best of the best. Before I joined, I told the Navy recruiter I wanted to take the SEAL Challenge. It guaranteed me the opportunity to become a candidate and I wasn't about to waste my chance when my time came.

Oddly enough, it was during BUD/S when I moved past my prejudice against the wealthy. I didn't have a choice when Brody Slater blew all my preconceived notions out of the water.

Everyone knew his story since the exploits landing him in the military were in the newspapers. He was the spoiled rich kid whose older brother used their wealth to bail him out of yet another mess when he was a junior in college. Except, that time, he'd royally screwed up by hacking into a government computer system and the prosecutor wanted to make an example out of him. The best his brother's lawyers could do was get them to agree to military enlistment instead of prison. How he managed to qualify for SEAL training was a mystery to me since one of the requirements was having a clean record. Sometimes they granted a waiver, which I assumed meant his brother pulled strings for him—again. Though, it didn't really matter. No one could help him through the training and I didn't think he had the mental toughness to make it.

When we were paired together as swim buddies on day one, I was pissed right the hell off. I knew I had what it took to be a damn good SEAL, but that didn't mean I wanted to be saddled with Brody.

The number one rule was to never leave your buddy behind and having him as my buddy was bound to be a major liability. When I first saw him, there was no doubt in my mind he would be one of many to ring the bell and signal their defeat. Not only was I going to have to make sure I never rang that damn bell, I would need to stand between him and it anytime he was ready to call it quits.

Quickly, I realized he wanted this as badly as I did and I was never so happy to be proved wrong in my life. Brody was the one who figured out the trick that helped us both survive. We got four meals a day, one every six hours. After our first day, Brody started to measure our time in meals. We pushed hard with one goal in mind: making it to the next meal. After a couple days, we were both operating on auto-pilot, focused on each six-hour block of time, pushing hard until we made it through the final day. He more than earned my respect and blew my misconceptions out of the water.

His skills on the keyboard had saved our asses on more than one mission—something I later realized the Navy had counted on when they gave him the chance to become a SEAL. I could ask Brody for anything and there was no doubt in my mind he'd either get me what I needed or die trying.

"You know you're going to owe me an explanation later, right?" Brody asked, drawing my attention back to the problem at hand.

"I know."

I heard the sound of typing in the background. "Found someone. I'm sending you contact information now."

"Thanks."

"You need me to meet you in Atlanta?" he asked.

I had no idea what was going on with Serena, but I knew what it took for Brody to make that offer. I didn't want him to leave Vegas unless it was absolutely necessary. "Hold tight for now. I'll let you know once I get there."

"Does Damian know you're heading out?"

"Not yet," I answered. "I'll talk to him after Serena has what she needs. I'll let you know more once I know the plan."

As soon as I hung up, Brody's text was waiting for me. I forwarded it to Serena.

Me: Call this guy ASAP. He'll help you until I can get there.

Serena: Got it.

Me: WTF is going on?

Serena: Not sure it's safe to text. Tell you when I see you.

Me: I'm overseas. It will take me about 24 hours to get there.

I waited a few minutes, but there was no reply. I figured she had either turned her phone off or was giving the guy a call. With that taken care of, I needed to talk to my boss—Brody's big brother, Damian.

Even though Brody and I were as close as brothers, six years passed before I met Damian. At the time, I was flat on my back in a naval hospital with Brody in the bed next to me. Our last mission had been fucked up beyond belief. Brody had been riding shotgun when we were hit by an IED. I'd been in the back of the humvee and was thrown clear of the wreckage. By the time I made it back to my team, three of our teammates were dead and Brody was hanging on by a thread. We were less than half a mile from our extraction point and I managed to carry him to the helo before taking a round to the knee as I was climbing on board.

When I awoke in the hospital, my injuries weren't as bad as Brody's, but we both knew we were going to be found unfit for duty. Brody's doctors had already sent a summary of his condition and records over to the nearest designated medical treatment facility. Mine were on their way since I was going to undergo knee replacement surgery. Damn bullet to the knee completely fucked it up and blew my chances to stay with the teams.

Eventually, Damian wanted to take his brother home and get him the best medical care possible, but Brody wasn't willing to leave without me. Once he told his brother I'd saved his life, Damian was more than willing to smooth the way for me to be discharged at the same time. The next few months were eye-opening for me. I had an up close and personal view into the lives of the rich and famous.

Damian attracted attention wherever he went. He liked to take chances and risked a decent amount of the family fortune to build a casino on the strip in Las Vegas a few years back. The gamble paid off when the resort became wildly popular, but it put them in the public eye more than Brody wanted. It wasn't a problem when he was rarely home, but now he just wanted to be left alone while he struggled with his rehabilitation and learned how to deal with people's reactions to the scars on his face.

People wanted what the Slaters had and being accessible meant Damian was the one in the crosshairs. It didn't help that Brody had become a paranoid motherfucker. The security around Damian was good—the best money could buy. But Brody knew there were men who were trained better, those who would put his life before theirs. Men who had served their country with a blind loyalty that was hard to find. And he wanted the best for his brother.

When my recovery was complete and I started looking for a job, Brody asked his brother to hire me as the head of his personal security. He didn't have to push hard to get him to say yes and with the salary Damian offered, it was a no-brainer for me to accept. A strange path brought me to where I was today: a casino in Monte Carlo, dressed in a tux, while Damian played a high-stakes game of poker for more money than I made in a year—which was a hell of a lot of money.

Heading over to the table, I turned my attention to each of the players before focusing on my boss. His pile of chips had steadily grown over the last couple hours. I had enough experience watching him play over the last year to know it wasn't going to be much longer before he'd walk away from the game victorious. I motioned to the two guards traveling with us, preparing them to be ready to leave soon, before moving to stand silently behind him. I waited until the current hand was finished before tapping him on the shoulder—our signal there was a problem that couldn't wait.

Damian leaned back in his chair, tilting his head so I could whisper in his ear. "I have a personal emergency and need to head back to the States."

Surprised by my words, he swiveled in his seat to stare at me silently for a moment. "I was beginning to think you didn't have a personal life," he murmured.

"Fuck off," I grumbled.

"Is that any way to talk to the man who's going to let you borrow his private jet?" he joked before raising a finger, gesturing 'one minute'. Turning back to the table, he focused on cards he was dealt and the other players as the round proceeded. After a few minutes, he pushed his pile of chips into the center. "All in."

Every player folded but one. When Damian turned over his cards to reveal a full house with kings and nines, the last remaining player swore before shoving back from the table to storm away. I couldn't help but hope Damian's streak of good luck held true for me—and Serena.

CHAPTER 2

Delia

The End...

Typing those two little words always left me feeling bittersweet. A mixture of relief for finishing on schedule—although it was quite often in the nick of time—sadness for feeling like I was saying goodbye to close friends, and a hint of guilt since I had no right being upset. As impossible as it was for me to believe sometimes, I had the best job in the world, the one I'd dreamed about since I was a little girl.

All those years of imagining tall tales and having my nose stuck in a book paid off when I finally sat down at my laptop to write my own. Now I spent my days creating romantic stories filled with alpha males and happily-ever-afters. As if that wasn't enough, I spent my nights reading them, too. My life revolved around the written word and I couldn't be happier—except when it came to meeting men.

Not the fictitious ones who lived in my head—I had plenty of those—it was meeting real life guys that presented a problem. Apparently, you needed to leave the house to find them, preferably not looking like you've just spent a week living under a rock—which is exactly what happened when I disappeared into my writing cave. The bottom line was, I had been too focused on my writing career and hadn't made time for dating lately.

Even if I had, once you factored in my impossibly high standards, you had the perfect recipe for a lengthy dry spell. I blamed it on reading so many romance novels growing up. I wanted a man my body craved, someone who made my heart beat faster with just one look, a look that said I was the only woman in the world. Fidelity, passion, and love...*was I really asking for too much?*

I also needed to add another feeling to the list: lonely. Most people wouldn't understand how I could miss people who only lived in my head, but saying goodbye to them wasn't easy. Doing it after spending two weeks completely by myself didn't help the situation at all. Logically, I knew coming up to the cabin to submerse myself into writing was my choice, but I wasn't thinking with my head right now—I was thinking with my heart. And my heart felt the pang of loneliness more than usual due to so many days of solitude.

Writing was a solitary profession and in my case, that probably wasn't a good thing since I tended to be an introvert. Usually, I needed time alone to recharge my batteries, but after locking myself away from society to get this book done, what I really needed was to talk to my best friend. I knew she'd be able to pull me out of my funk and help me get my head straight before I hit the road in the morning. She'd been doing it practically our whole lives. Walking over to the table in the entryway where I'd left my purse the day I arrived, I dug through it, looking for my cell phone.

"Crap," I swore under my breath, even though there wasn't anyone around to hear my bad language. I had thrown my phone in there at my last stop for gas on the way up, thinking I'd powered it off. It was right after I posted to all my social media profiles, letting everyone know I was going to be out of reach for a couple weeks. It had been crunch time and I needed to get away from any and all distractions if I was going to finish before my deadline. The cabin was the perfect getaway spot since it didn't have internet access and cell service was spotty in the mountains. Only...it was a little too perfect in this instance. There wasn't a landline and I hadn't bothered to pack my charger since I knew I wasn't going to be using my phone.

A quick glance out the window told me it was too late to leave for home. It wasn't a good idea to traverse the mountain roads at night, especially without a functioning phone. Now I felt especially dumb for not going into the Volkswagen dealership to have them look at the built-in phone charger that broke a couple months ago. The car wasn't due for an oil change for another couple months; I figured it could wait until then. This was yet another example of how my procrastination almost always came back to bite me in the butt at the worst time possible.

But it wasn't like there was anything I could do about it now. I had never been one to believe in pity parties and refused to sit and pout. There was a bottle of wine in the fridge with my name on it, some cream puffs in the freezer I could defrost as a treat, and several books waiting for me on my kindle. It looked like I needed to pull up my big girl panties and make the best of a bad situation.

One quick glance around the room made me realize my plans to unwind needed to wait. I was always a bit of a slob, but the cabin looked like a tornado had come through since I arrived. Or maybe I should just chalk it up to Hurricane Delia since I was the one responsible for the empty wrappers, paper plates, and plastic cups piled onto just about every available surface. Cleaning was the last thing I wanted to do, but I made myself do it anyway. It kept me busy for a little while and took my mind off being alone. Plus, it needed to be done before I left.

After taking a long shower and starting a fire in the fireplace in my bedroom, I climbed into bed. I wouldn't be ready to fall asleep for a few hours yet, but I had my wine and cream puffs waiting on the nightstand and my kindle on the bed. Thumbing through the books I downloaded before leaving home, I had a difficult time choosing which to read first. My eyes kept going back to a romantic suspense with a shy heroine and the military man who swept her off her feet and out of danger. The story called to me on a deeper level and I decided to start with it.

A few hours later, I found myself wiping tears from my cheeks after reading a touching proposal in the epilogue. As I turned off the light and rolled over to hug my pillow, I couldn't stop myself from wishing I had someone to hug instead. It would be nice if the stories I wrote and read came true in real life. I would give just about anything to have an alpha hero of my own.

CHAPTER 3

Blaine

Flying on a private jet definitely had its advantages—like being able to use my phone. The moment the plane was within cell tower range, a text from Serena came through.

Serena: Meet me for lunch at the place we last saw each other.

The wording of her text bothered me. It was cryptic enough to let me know she was scared about revealing too much information, hinting at the possibility of her messages being traced. Luckily, the Hilton, where I'd stayed the last time I was in Atlanta, was only about a twenty minute cab ride from the airport, depending on traffic. I sent her a quick text letting her know I'd be there. I also sent Brody a message, filling him in on the plan. His response was swift and succinct, another offer to hop on a plane if I needed him.

Unfortunately, the same couldn't be said for Serena. By the time I landed, she still hadn't responded. The last contact I'd had with her, aside from the cryptic one, was last night when she confirmed she had received the information for Brody's contact. If she'd managed

23

to check in to the Hilton, then he must have come through for her. I needed to focus on getting there as quickly as possible. Without knowing what the hell was going on, I couldn't be certain how long she'd be safe at the hotel.

It was lunch time when I arrived, almost a full twenty-four hours since I received Serena's first message. The hotel's lobby was fairly busy, but I didn't see any sign of her. Heading into the restaurant where we'd had dinner years ago, I hoped like hell she was already waiting. I scanned the restaurant, quickly realizing I had beat her there.

"Table for two. In the corner," I instructed the hostess, choosing the seat facing the entrance.

After about thirty minutes of waiting, I took pity on my waitress and ordered a burger. Checking my cell every couple of minutes or so, I started getting antsy after another half hour passed. So far, the only thing I had managed to accomplish was a full stomach. Leaning back in my chair, my gaze drifted over the room again. It was much busier than it had been a few years ago. Possibly even abnormally busy for a hotel restaurant in the middle of the week.

"Seems like a full house," I murmured to my waitress as she came over to clear my plate. I'd caught her eyes drifting down to check out my body a few times already, so I flashed her a smile, making her blush. If I needed to use her attraction to me to get some information, then that's what I was going to do. "Is there a convention or something in town?"

She looked around before leaning forward to whisper her response. "It sounds crazy, but I think a lot of them are gawkers."

"Gawkers?" I repeated.

"Yeah, they probably saw the news about that author who was murdered here this morning and came for lunch to find out if there was anything to see," she explained. "It's heartless, is what it is. That poor woman deserves better than this after what happened to her."

"I hadn't heard the news." My reply surprised her and I hurried to explain, not wanting to lose a valuable source of information. "I was overseas until today. This was my first stop after my plane landed."

"Oh, I guess that makes sense." She looked at the unused place setting across from me. "Was your friend delayed?"

"Looks that way," I confirmed.

Her eyes flicked to the empty chair and back to mine again. "If it's a date, then she's crazy for standing you up."

"Not a date," I corrected. "Just a friend."

She blushed again, but I didn't feel the pull of attraction. Although she was pretty, she wasn't my type, even if the timing had been perfect. I was sure there were plenty of guys who would have been happy to have the tall blonde hit on them, but I wasn't one of them. I rarely went after blondes and I liked my women with more curves. "Somebody was really murdered here?"

She looked up to make sure nobody was listening to our conversation and took another step closer. "That's what I heard, but my friend, who was working this morning, said the police wouldn't say who it was or if she really was murdered when they questioned her. Rumor has it the maid who found the body said she was beaten and shot several times, including in the face. I don't see how it could be anything but murder."

"And nobody heard anything?"

She leaned forward, her breasts right in my face, and whispered in my ear. "The maid also said she was tied up and had a gag in her mouth, but I'm not supposed to talk about it. The manager lectured us about how to handle the situation before my shift started. I really shouldn't have said anything, but you seem like a trustworthy guy."

As badly as I wanted to grill her for more information, I knew by the look on her face and the quiver in her voice there was no way she was going to say anything else. "My lips are sealed."

She left the check and I stuck some cash inside the holder. Enough time had passed that I needed to consider the possibility of Serena not showing up. I sent Brody a quick text asking him to get in touch with his contact to see if he had any information and then I pulled up my web browser to look for the news stories the waitress had mentioned. There it was—local author found murdered in hotel room.

The article didn't include many details, just her name, a little bit about her career, and the basics about her death. The lack of information wasn't surprising considering it had only been half a day since her body was discovered. I didn't know if there was any kind of connection, but I didn't like the coincidence of Serena choosing to hide in a hotel where a murder took place.

Right now, I felt like my hands were tied. I had no idea where Serena was or where she lived, so looking for her was also out. The way I saw it, I had three options: ask Brody for another favor, call my mom, or wait to see if Serena showed. It really was a no-brainer. Without any intel on the situation, I didn't want to sit here with my thumb up my ass and there was no way in hell I was going to get my mom involved—and not just because it was dangerous. If she knew I'd been in touch with Serena again, she'd start plotting to get us back together. Between her friendship with Serena's mom and her recent hints that I wasn't getting any younger, she would take this as a sign from up above to plan a wedding or some crazy shit like that. That left me with one viable option.

Me: Can you find an address for Serena?
Brody: You flew halfway around the world for her and you don't even know where she lives?

I wasn't surprised he was busting my balls about this. If our roles were reversed, I'd be doing the same thing. It didn't mean I had to like it, though.

Me: Can you do it or not?
Brody: Chill out. Already done. Sending it now.

I waited another ten minutes, watching as the restaurant emptied from the lunch rush. Although Serena hadn't specified a time for us to meet, if I

27

waited much longer, I was going to draw attention to myself, and that was the last thing I wanted to do.

Grabbing a cab, I gave the driver the address Brody had sent over and used the drive over to search the internet for any news connected to the hotel in the last day other than the author's murder. When my search didn't turn anything up, I googled Serena's name. The only things I found were some social media profiles and photos of her with the guy I assumed she was dating. I made a mental note of his name and memorized his face for future reference.

The photos weren't from too long ago, yet she had come to me for help instead of him. It could be because she knew I was better equipped to handle dangerous situations and she didn't want him to get hurt, or he was part of the reason she was running.

When the cabbie pulled up to Serena's place, I was surprised to find myself at an expensive looking townhome. "Keep the meter running," I instructed him as I stepped out of the cab. Knowing it was a long shot, I walked up to the front door and rang the bell.

A part of me hoped Serena would answer and tell me she'd overreacted and everything was fine. After minute or two had passed, I knew that wasn't going to happen. I looked down at the welcome mat on the front step and wondered if she'd picked up the same habit her mom had when we were growing up. It was an idiotic thing to do living in Atlanta, but Serena never was one to think things all the way through.

I glanced at the cabbie from the corner of my eye. He had pulled out a book and his attention wasn't focused on me, so I bent down and peeled back the upper left corner of the rug. And there it was. A goddamn key to her front door. If Serena had been standing in front of me, I would have shaken her in fury for taking such a stupid risk with her safety—even though her mistake meant I was able to let myself into her house.

Finding the key turned out to be a good thing. Someone had been here before me, tossing the place. Couch cushions ripped open, drawers all dumped out, everything from her bookshelves tossed into a pile on the floor. Odds were damn good they were looking for something specific. The bad news was I had no fucking clue what it could be. The state of her apartment combined with her no-show at the hotel was most likely the first signs that this situation was going to be fucked beyond all recognition.

I had no way of knowing if the damage had been done before or after Serena ran. I tried calling her number, but she still wasn't picking up. My only other option for information seemed to be Brody's contact. Luckily, Brody picked up on the first try.

"Serena didn't show at the hotel and her place has been searched. What did your contact have to say?" I asked before he could say hello.

"I haven't been able to reach him." His answer was the last thing I wanted to hear.

"Fuck!" Operating without any information was the surest way to end up hurt—or dead. "Where can I find him?"

"He's not answering his phone and hasn't responded to the message I left him on his eepSite."

"In English, Hack," I demanded. He knew I hated when he reverted to geek-speak. It flew straight over my head most of the time.

"I don't have a physical address for him. Our communication has all been done through phone calls and his website. It's an I2P site, which means it's anonymously hosted. I've already started digging, but it looks like he's running servers in multiple locations. It will take time, but I'll be able to pull an identity eventually," he explained.

It was still over my head, but I knew Brody would find this guy if it was doable. "What about his phone? Can you trace him through it faster?"

"Looks like it's a burner. One he only started using a week ago and hasn't used since about six hours after Serena called him."

"I've got a cab waiting for me. I guess I'll head back to the hotel and hope like hell she shows up this time," I muttered. "While I'm stuck here twiddling my thumbs, can you run a background check on Serena? If she doesn't show up soon, I'm going to have to start finding people who know her and asking questions to see if I can figure out what the fuck is going on."

"Want me to check police reports for the last day? See if someone reported her missing?"

He wouldn't limit his search to missing persons reports and we both knew it. I was already frustrated as hell and the thought of finding out something horrible happened to Serena after she asked me for help pushed all the wrong buttons. I hated being in the dark, stuck searching through her things for clues. Grabbing one of the books from the floor, I threw it against the wall before answering Brody's question. "Yes."

The book didn't fare well. The cover was torn and I felt like shit when I flipped through the first couple pages and realized it had been signed by the author. The guys who had torn her place apart had done enough damage, I didn't need to add to it. As I walked over to the bookshelf to set it down, the name on the cover jumped out at me. "Shit," I hissed.

"You about to get caught?"

"I didn't have to break in. I found her spare key hidden exactly where her mom used to leave hers when we were growing up," I explained

His bark of laughter was full of disbelief. "She's on the run from God only knows what kind of trouble and she didn't even bother to grab the spare key?"

"Nope," I confirmed.

"Then if I don't need to be worried about bailing your ass out of jail, what's wrong?"

"What do you think the odds are of Serena having an autographed copy of a book by an author whose body was found at the same hotel I was supposed to meet her at today?"

"I'd say there's no such thing as coincidence."

Digging through the pile of books, I found several others written by the same person. "I just found five more of them. Every single one has a personalized message inside addressed to Serena."

"Maybe the author's connected to Serena's problem somehow?" Brody suggested.

"It's worth looking into, especially since I don't have anything else to go on right now. I need to get back outside before the cabbie gets curious. The last thing I need is to find myself stuck at the police station," I said, heading to the front door. "Can you get me an address for Delia Sinclair? The article I found online said she was a local author."

"You gonna break into two homes on the same day, Saint?" Brody asked. I was sure his use of my nickname was deliberate since I had a reputation for being a stickler for the rules. It used to drive him nuts since Brody was the kind of guy who hated rules. "Maybe I rubbed off on you more than we realized."

"Blow me," I mumbled. "I don't know what I'm going to do yet, but until I get in touch with Serena or you get ahold of your guy, she's the only lead I have."

"You do realize if she's a murder victim and the police are working her case, they're most likely going to spend some time in her neighborhood investigating, right?"

"I've managed to get our team into tighter spaces," I argued.

"I wouldn't recommend using C4 today. The cops might notice."

"Thanks for the advice, Mr. Obvious," I growled. "Just get me the address, okay?"

"It's already on the way to you. And while I'm at it, I think I might just do a little exploring in the Atlanta police department's network to see what I can find."

"How about you spend more time worrying about not getting caught hacking into their system and less time worrying about me breaking and entering?" I grumbled. "It's not like Damian can hook you up with the same deal as last time."

I regretted my words the minute they left my mouth. Neither of us had been ready to leave the teams when we had, but Brody was having a harder time adjusting to civilian life. I wasn't able to be a SEAL anymore, but it didn't take me long to recover from my knee replacement surgery. Brody was still struggling with his injuries and it had left him feeling bitter.

"Shit, man. I'm sorry," I apologized.

His silence had me wondering if he was going to hang up. "It's okay, Saint. Just be careful out there. I know this is personal for you, but you need to distance yourself and treat it like any other mission. Find Serena, get her out of whatever trouble she's landed herself in, and get out."

"Sounds like a plan," I agreed, but it was pointless since he'd already hung up on me.

I hopped into the cab and gave the driver the author's address. During the ride, I went back online to check for any more stories about her death. Still no statement from the police and no updates to any of the stories already out there. I felt like I was batting zero when it came to finding intel on the situation. I did a quick search of the author as we entered her neighborhood, finding her website and Facebook page.

Her last update was about ten days ago, saying she was going to be out of touch for a couple weeks while she was finishing up a manuscript. Apparently, she was checked into a hotel less than thirty minutes from her house to get away from everyone. I wondered if she managed to finish the book before someone killed her and hoped like hell her house would give me a lead on what happened to Serena.

As we entered her neighborhood, I asked the cabbie to drop me off about a mile from her house. The houses were nicer than I expected—being an author must have paid better than I thought. The further I walked, the bigger the lots were. Once I got a couple houses down from her place, the first thing I noticed was the cop car parked out front.

When I saw the 'for sale' sign in the yard across the street, I headed in that direction, playing the interested buyer. Peering into the windows in front and walking around to the back yard, I kept my attention split between the vacant home and the one across the street. The opportunity to gather intel was too good to pass up. When the cops headed back to their car, I made sure I was rounding the corner of the yard. They came from her neighbor's house and changed direction as soon as they noticed me.

"Good afternoon, officers," I greeted them, trying to look as harmless as possible. It wasn't an easy thing to do when you were six-foot-three of solid muscle, but it was worth a shot.

The younger one approached me. If I had to guess, I would have said he only had a few years on the job. "Good afternoon, sir. We'd like to ask you a few questions."

"Anything you need, officer. I'm not sure I'll be of any help since I just flew in today on business. I'm looking at some houses for my boss over the next few days." I wanted to make sure I crossed myself off their suspect list immediately by making it clear I couldn't have murdered the author since I had been on an airplane. Using Damian as my excuse for house shopping bought me time if they wanted to look deeper. He was almost impossible to reach by phone unless he wanted to take your call. And if I asked him to be unavailable, then he'd make sure it happened until Brody and I could build a cover story for why Damian would have sent me to Atlanta.

The cops took down my information after asking me a few more questions. I was surprised when they headed back to their car and left. It looked like luck was on my side, after all. I wasn't familiar with police procedure, but it seemed odd they weren't leaving someone behind to watch her house. Then again, I'd never been involved in a murder investigation before, so what the hell did I know? They head probably already searched her house. At least, I hoped they had. It would be damn inconvenient if they came back while I was inside.

If I were doing my job as lead breacher overseas in a war zone, I could just blow my way into the house in question. Not today, though. I was in the middle of a suburban neighborhood and needed to get inside without drawing unwanted attention. If I got caught, I'd have a hell of a time explaining what I was doing since I was operating outside the law on a mission I'd basically given myself. On the plus side, at least I couldn't be court-martialled since I wasn't in the Navy anymore.

Luckily for me, Ms. Sinclair didn't have one of those security system signs in front of her house like so many in the neighborhood did. It wasn't a guarantee she didn't have one, but it upped the odds in my favor. As I strolled past her place, I also noted the privacy fence and tree line made her backyard private. Not the usual I-don't-want-my-neighbors-peaking-into-my-windows private, but the I-want-to-be-in-my-backyard-and-pretend-nobody-lives-near-me private. That boded well for me, too.

When I doubled back and nobody was outside, it was too much of a temptation to pass up. I headed for the gate I spied in the privacy fence. A quick squeeze of the handle told me the author was seriously lax with her security. She'd made it public knowledge that she was going to be out of town for two weeks and then didn't even bother to lock the gate to her yard. It looked like she was fucking clueless to the dangers out there—something that might have resulted in her murder.

Pushing that morbid thought aside, I got down to business, looking for clues. The place wasn't what I'd call clean—it certainly wouldn't pass the white glove test—but she wasn't a complete slob.

As I searched through drawers and closets, I discovered she was a bit of a hoarder though, which made the search more difficult. It seemed like her favored method of cleaning was to dump stuff out of sight. Other than a mess, I wasn't having any luck finding a single clue to how deep her connection was to Serena or what shit she was involved in that would make someone want to kill her.

By the time it had gotten dark outside, I had just about given up on finding anything. I still hadn't heard anything from Serena, and Brody's background check on Delia Sinclair didn't turn up a single thing out of the ordinary.

The sound of the garage door going up startled me, setting me into motion. It was a good thing I had been trained to make split second decisions with limited information because that skill set was being put to the test right now. I moved toward the kitchen as I ran the possible scenarios through my head. If it was Serena using a friend's place to lay low, then I was in the clear. If it was a boyfriend or family member of the dead author, I was probably screwed. A cleaning person or friend, I might be okay. The bottom line was, I had no way of knowing which scenario I was about to face, but it didn't matter. There wasn't a chance in hell I was going out the back without knowing if the person walking through that door was Serena.

Right as my decision was made, I heard the sound of the garage door lowering, quickly followed by the door connecting the garage to the house opening and closing. A deep feminine sigh resonated, but I stayed in position on the other side of the refrigerator and out of sight. The sound of footsteps got closer and then a woman entered the kitchen. I hadn't meant to make a noise, but I shifted as soon as I realized who was standing in front of me. I moved toward her so I could cover her mouth and get her under control before she screamed and one of the neighbors came to see what was wrong. And holy fuck, there was plenty wrong with this situation since the woman was supposed to be dead.

My heart fell at the realization of what seeing her alive meant for Serena. *Someone* had checked into the

Hilton last night as Delia Sinclair and was killed in that hotel room this morning. With Serena nowhere to be found and Delia standing in front of me, there was only one conclusion I could make: it was Serena's body they had found.

Seeing Delia for the first time in person, I understood why Serena might have chosen to use her identity. The resemblance hadn't been clear in the photo from the newspaper article, but they were both approximately five-foot-six with curvy figures. Delia's hair was only a couple shades darker than Serena's had been. She was exactly my type and I couldn't help but notice how gorgeous she was. It was completely inappropriate considering the situation, but my groin tightened with need and I had to wrangle it back.

This was about as wrong a time as any for me to lust after a woman. The thought crossed my mind that I probably just needed to get laid, but I ruthlessly pushed it away, too. Instead, I focused on the woman's delicate features, the shadows under her eyes, the vulnerability shining brightly from them like a beacon. Odds were damn good she was an innocent in this whole damn mess—someone in the wrong place at the wrong time. I couldn't let it matter to me, though. The fact of the matter was she was already a part of this clusterfuck. The second Serena checked into a hotel under her name, she was involved. And if Serena had been able to pass for Delia, then the opposite was true and I just might have to use her as bait to draw the bad guys out.

CHAPTER 4

Delia

I didn't even have time to react to the sight of a stranger in my house before I was grabbed. His hand covered my mouth as I tried to scream, making it come out more like a muffled yelp. I struggled against his hold, frantic to get away—to find help. If I were anything like the heroines in my books, I would know how to free myself with some fancy self-defense moves. Unfortunately, I wasn't the least bit athletic and would probably hurt myself. Still, I wasn't going to give up without a fight of some kind. A self-inflicted injury had to be better than whatever he planned to do with me.

Unable to break free from his hold or scream for help, I was quickly growing more frantic. My heart felt like it was about to jump out of my chest. Tears of frustration streamed down my cheeks. My muffled yelps had quickly turned to frightened whimpers as a litany of regrets tumbled through my mind.

If only I hadn't drunk the entire bottle of wine last night.

If only I had left the cabin earlier, I would have been home with my lights blazing—a clear deterrent to a burglar casing my neighborhood.

If only I had that damn security system installed like I kept planning to do instead of putting it off.

If only…

"I'm not here to hurt you." My whirling thoughts stopped and my body stilled at the sound of his voice—a low rumble I found oddly soothing. "It's my fault you're scared right now and I've given you no reason to trust me—I get that. But I need you to give me a chance to explain. Can you do that?"

I nodded frantically, desperate to believe he was telling me the truth. If not, I was in trouble. There was no way I could defend myself against this guy. The arms wrapped around my body were roped with muscle and he towered over me by at least half a foot. I wasn't a small woman by any means of the imagination, but I felt tiny against his massive chest.

"I'm going to pull my hand away now, but you have to promise not to scream. If you do, I'm going to have to do something to keep you quiet," he warned. I nodded again, even though I knew I'd scream if it were my only option. Doing something was better than doing nothing. "You really don't want me to have to do that."

His last words were gruffly spoken in a guttural tone, sending shivers up my spine. I had no idea what this man would do to ensure I didn't yell and I had a feeling I never wanted to know—especially if it meant experiencing it firsthand. I forced myself to relax, nodding my head once more to let him know I understood the threat and took it seriously.

He moved us closer to the kitchen table and I heard a clattering noise as his foot hooked a chair to pull it away from the table. I felt stark relief at the loosening of his hold until his hands gripped my arms as he pushed me down to sit. When he yanked another chair out and sat next to me, he was close enough that my legs pressed against his.

My jaw almost dropped open as I got my first good look at him. If I had to conjure up an image of an intruder, he was the last thing I would come up with on my own. On the other hand, if I was putting pen to paper and building a character description for one of my heroes, he'd fit perfectly. He had tall, dark, and dangerous down to a tee. His dark brown hair was cut short, almost in a military style, but a tad longer. My fingers practically twitched with the desire to run them over his head to see if it would feel bristly or soft against my palm. Piercing blue eyes were a startling contrast to his tanned skin and the ridiculously long eyelashes framing them were the only feminine thing about him, though it didn't do much to soften the brutal masculinity of his face.

My eyes lowered, drifting down his body. His dark blue Henley stretched taught across his chest with the sleeves pushed up mid-arm. There was no wonder why his arms had felt so strong around me. If I tried to wrap both my hands around his bicep, I wasn't sure they would touch.

Muscular thighs strained against the material of his jeans and he finished off the look with black military-style boots that looked like they had to be a size thirteen, at least. At the inappropriate thought that jumped into my head about what else his shoe size might mean, I jerked my gaze back up guiltily. Damn, but this guy was potent. He'd just broken into my house and subdued me like it was nothing, yet here I was, checking him out and wondering about the size of his dick.

"Who are you?" I whispered.

"You don't know me," he began, stating the obvious. If I'd met him before, there was no way I'd be asking him who he was now. He wasn't the type of guy a woman ever forgot. "But we have a friend in common. Serena Foster."

The name didn't ring any bells for me, but that wasn't a huge surprise since I was horrible at remembering names. One thing I knew for certain, she wasn't a close friend. I didn't have many of those. So, either she was more of an acquaintance or he had the wrong house...and the wrong woman.

"Serena Foster?" I repeated the name.

"Shit," he muttered before reaching into his pocket and yanking a cell phone out. I wasn't sure why, but I sat there, waiting, instead of trying to get away while he was distracted. He swiped a finger across the screen, messed with it for a minute or so, and then turned the screen my way. "Yeah, this is her."

I recognized her face as soon as I saw the photo. "I wouldn't call her a friend. She came to a signing a couple months ago."

"A signing?"

"I'm an author, she reads my books. We talked for a little bit, but those things are always so busy. We didn't get the chance to chat for long," I explained. "Why would you think we were friends?"

"I found the books at her place. Looks like I put two and two together and came up with five."

"I don't understand," I mumbled. "Why didn't you just ask her about me? Why break into my house like this?"

"Fuck," he hissed, dropping his steely gaze for a moment before locking his eyes with mine again. "Don't freak out, but according to news reports, you died last night at the Hilton Downtown."

My breath seized in my lungs at his words. I couldn't believe what he was saying. It just didn't make any sense. When I looked into his eyes, they seemed to be filled with honesty and determination. How was that possible? He had just broken into my home and was obviously off his rocker.

"Died?" I repeated dumbly. "Why in the world would anyone think I was dead? I haven't even stayed at the Hilton in months."

The next thing I knew, he pulled up a newspaper article and handed me his phone so I could read it. The headline jumped out at me: *Local Author Found Murdered at Hilton Downtown*. The story was brief, without a lot of details. Apparently, a member of the hotel staff had leaked the name of the guest since the police had been quoted as saying the investigation was ongoing and the victim's identity hadn't been confirmed. And there was no denying it was my name they'd leaked. A hysterical giggle bubbled up as I read the line a second time. Apparently, I had been wrong—he wasn't the one off their rocker here, I was.

"The victim's identity hasn't been confirmed," I whispered, hardly able to believe my own eyes.

"The police were here this afternoon, asking your neighbors questions. Odds are they were told you were away from home working on a book. Which could fit with you being checked into a hotel," he pointed out. "Right now, they don't have any reason to think it's not your body lying in the morgue."

"And you think it was Serena, don't you?" I asked disbelievingly. This whole situation was surreal—a perfect case of the truth being stranger than fiction. I couldn't come up with a storyline like this if I tried.

"I do," he confirmed. "She was in trouble and needed a safe place to stay. I think she checked into that hotel under your name last night."

"But why would she pick my name to use?" I cried.

He looked down at his phone and flipped back to her photo. "My best guess is she was desperate and knew how much she looked like you."

As crazy as it sounded, he could be right about that. "We joked about it," I sighed. "When we took a photo of the two of us together, we both thought we could easily pass for sisters. I told her it would have been nice if it were true since I'm an only child and always wanted siblings. A big sister would have been perfect."

"And that's the only time the two of you met in person?" he asked.

"Yes, that's why this whole thing is insane. I don't even know her. I feel horrible that she might be dead, but I still don't understand why you're here. In my home. Uninvited," I clipped out.

"She called me a few days ago, said she was in trouble and needed my help," he started. I didn't let him get very far, though.

"If she was in the kind of trouble where she needed a fake identity and ended up getting murdered, why didn't she go to the police?" I asked. "What did she think you could do for her that they couldn't do?"

"Serena and I grew up next door to each other. Our moms are still friends. No matter how blessed our lives, how charmed our existence, things still inevitably go wrong. She knew I was the kind of guy you called when that happened. When she had nowhere else to turn, she knew all she had to do was contact me and I'd come running."

Score one for the dead woman. I sure as heck didn't have anyone like that in my life. Although, before this moment, I would have sworn my life was too boring to ever need someone running to my rescue. "And what makes you that guy?"

"I have the skills to help her, courtesy of the United States government. The best training a man can have."

"You're a soldier?"

"Not a soldier, a sailor," he corrected. "And even better than that, a SEAL."

"A Navy SEAL, huh?" I repeated on an exhale.

"I retired a year ago, but once a SEAL, always a SEAL," he confirmed.

I'd done a lot of research into SEALs for my books and knew it wasn't rare for men to claim the distinction even if they hadn't earned the right to do so. If he was telling the truth, I could almost understand why Serena reached out to him for help if she felt like her trouble was bad enough the police couldn't help. But I needed more information. I wasn't just going to blindly believe what he was telling me. "What's your name?"

"Blaine West."

"Where did you go through BUD/S?"

"Coronado."

"What class were you?"

"Class 275."

"Who was your swim buddy?"

"Brody Slater," he bit out before asking a question of his own. "Are we both going to get a chance to play twenty questions?"

I felt the heat creeping up my neck and across my cheeks, but I refused to be embarrassed. If anyone had a reason to feel uncomfortable here, it was him—not me. "No, I figure you probably did some checking into my background before you broke into my home. It's only fair I get to ask the questions now."

The muscles in his forearms bunched as he tightened his fists before opening his hands to rub them over his face. "What else do you want to know?"

So far, he'd answered my questions swiftly and decisively, without hesitation. He wasn't volunteering to show me a bogus tattoo of a trident that would prove he was a SEAL or anything stupid like that. It held the ring of truth and the name he offered rang a bell. "Your swim buddy? Is he who I think he is?"

"Depends on who you think he is, but probably," he muttered.

When the story about the younger Slater brother joining the Navy hit the newspapers, I'd been intrigued. I couldn't help but wonder what motivated a guy with his kind of wealth to become a hacker in the first place. It was so far outside my experience, I couldn't even begin to understand putting your freedom at risk like that. But I respected his decision to fight for his country instead of going to jail. The articles made him out to be a bit of a wild card. It wasn't too difficult to imagine someone like him would want to be a SEAL. And if Blaine was lying, it was incredibly stupid to use the name of someone like Brody Slater as his fictitious swim buddy.

"This is for real, isn't it? Serena asking you for help. The news article. All of it," I breathed out.

"I wish like hell I could tell you it wasn't, but I can't. The situation is all too real."

I started to tremble as it all sank in. A woman I'd met a few short months ago died this morning—was murdered and the police thought she was me. They had been here asking questions and were probably digging into my life at this very moment, trying to figure out why someone had wanted me dead. At that thought, I jumped out of my seat and ran to the calendar hanging on the wall. I frantically turned the page to the current month and breathed a sigh of relief when I saw the date circled in red was still a week away. "Oh, thank God," I sighed.

"You okay?" Blaine asked from behind me. He was standing so close, I could feel his body heat against my back.

I took a small step closer to the wall before turning, hoping to put a little space between us. "I wouldn't say I'm okay, but at least I don't have to worry about my parents freaking out because the police called them to tell them I was dead."

"Damn, I should have thought of that. Why isn't it a concern?"

I flicked my thumb over my shoulder, pointing at the calendar. "They're in the Mediterranean on a chartered yacht and won't be in port for another week. When I talked to them before I got to the cabin, they gave me their itinerary so I wouldn't worry. Usually they call me every week. I probably have a voicemail from them from a few days ago, but I won't be able to call them back until they're back on land again."

"Neither will the police," he murmured. "And I highly doubt they'd tell them you're dead without positive identification. They're more likely to ask them to come back to help with the investigation. Does anybody know you came back early?"

"No."

I could practically see the wheels turning in his head while he stared at me in silence. He nodded his head, seeming to come to a decision before he spoke again. "I don't like the idea of you staying here until I have more information about why Serena was in danger. Your house isn't a secure location and it's possible her actions might have put you in the crosshairs."

I glanced at the phone charger lying on my kitchen counter. "I'll call the police. I'm sure they will want to know about the mix-up. If they think I'm in danger, then I'll do whatever they tell me I need to do to stay safe."

"I can understand why you might think that's the best decision to make here, but I want you to consider another option. Give me a little bit of time—the four days you have before anyone expects you to be back—and let me dig into the situation before you go to the police. I'll take you somewhere secure. Keep you safe from harm," he promised.

"Do you really think I'm in danger?"

"Until I saw you walk through that door, I thought you were dead. I didn't know they'd killed Serena. Hell, I don't even know who *they* are," he muttered. "I might not know much about the situation right now, but it isn't a stretch of the imagination to think it's possible you might be in danger. And if you are, the safest place to be is with me."

For a guy willing to admit he didn't know what was going on, he certainly seemed confident in his own abilities. "I don't even know you! Why in the world would I trust you with my safety instead of the police?"

"I haven't seen Serena in years, but the girl I knew wasn't dumb. There had to have been a reason she didn't go to the police. Until I know why she made the decision to come to me for help instead, I have to operate under the assumption they might be involved."

When I woke up this morning, I was worried my life was too boring and I needed to do something to spice it up a little. Now, I was dealing with a stolen identity, a possible conspiracy theory, and a murder—not to mention, an incredibly hot ex-Navy SEAL. I needed to be careful what I wished for in the future. I was in way over my head.

First things first, no matter what I decided to do, I needed to charge my phone. I didn't have a landline and I was extremely aware that I had no way of calling for help without my cell. My purse was on the floor by the fridge where it must have fallen when I was struggling against Blaine earlier. I picked it up and got my phone out, plugging it into the charger and wishing like heck, once again, I'd remembered to bring it along with me to the cabin. If I had, I would have been able to answer it when the police most likely had called today. Instead, if they had called, it went straight to voicemail and just reinforced the idea that I was the victim of the murder they were investigating.

"There's no way I'm going somewhere with you unless I speak to someone who can confirm you are who you say you are first," I said.

"Seems fair to me," he agreed, turning his phone so I could see the screen as he pulled up his contacts list and pressed the call button for someone listed as "Hack".

Putting it on speakerphone, I listened as the phone rang once before a deep voice came through the line. "Any sign of Serena?"

The flare of pain in Blaine's eyes was unmistakable. "No, and I don't think I'm going to find one since Delia Sinclair is standing in front of me right now."

"Fucking A, man. Are you shitting me?"

"Speakerphone," Blaine warned, pressing his lips together in annoyance.

"Sorry."

There was an awkward silence and if I weren't listening, I knew they would both have a lot more to say to each other. Hearing the man ask about Serena eased some of my concern, but not all of it. "This is Delia Sinclair. Can you describe Blaine West to me?"

There was silence on the other end of the line. "Go ahead and answer her questions," Blaine said, giving the okay.

"Six-foot-three, two-hundred-twenty-five pounds, dark hair, blue eyes, muscular build."

The description he provided was spot on, but I needed more information. "How do you know him?"

"We served in the Navy together, ma'am."

His answer and the nickname helped me connect the dots in my brain. "Is this Brody Slater?"

"Yes, ma'am," he confirmed.

I glanced down at the screen and saw the Facetime button was an available option. I pressed it and waited for Brody to do the same on his end. It didn't take long before I saw a familiar face staring back at me.

"When did you meet each other?"

"First Phase training to become a SEAL," he replied.

"Thank you," I whispered, nodding my acceptance of this conversation as confirmation that Blaine really was who he said he was.

I zoned out as they talked for a couple more minutes and was startled when I felt Blaine's hand wrap around my arm. When I looked up, his phone was nowhere in sight and he was looking at me in concern, his brow furrowed. "Anything else I can do to make you feel more comfortable about leaving with me?" he asked.

"As a matter of fact, there is. I'd be insane to go anywhere with you when the police think I'm dead and you're the only person who knows they're wrong, except for your friend. If I'm going to give you some time to do your thing before I contact the police, then I need to call my best friend to let her know I'm with you," I insisted.

The approving smile he flashed me made my heart flutter. "That's a smart move on your part."

"And I don't just mean your name. Give me your driver's license," I ordered, holding my hand out.

It calmed my nerves further when he pulled his wallet out of his back pocket and handed me his license without arguing. Luckily, my phone had charged just enough that it had powered back on. I took a picture of it and then snapped a quick picture of him since he looked different now. His hair was shorter and his face a little fuller—he looked healthier now.

I tapped out a quick message to Mila, letting her know I was okay and that I needed her to call me as soon as she was available. Then I forwarded both pictures to her, knowing darn well it would light a fire under her and get her to call me even faster than usual. She'd be way too excited by the fact that I'd met a hot guy to wait a moment longer than necessary to get the details from me. Sending her a picture of Blaine was like waving a red flag in front of a bull.

After that was done, I pulled the internet up and searched for the story Blaine had showed me on his phone earlier. I wasn't sure whether I wanted to really find it or not. If it was there, then this was all real. If not, it was an elaborate ruse—one which made no sense at all. As I waited for the results of the search, I debated internally which situation would be preferable. Then it no longer mattered. Several stories popped up.

"I'm not lying," he said quietly, looking over my shoulder at my phone.

"I needed to be sure," I explained.

"Have you worked through your doubts?"

I squeezed my eyes shut, fighting against the tears that had sprung unexpectedly at the gentleness of his tone. "Yes."

His hands felt warm and strong as he rested them on my shoulders and lightly squeezed. "Once you walk out that door with me, you need to leave all your uncertainty about me behind. Trusting me is imperative if I'm going to be able to keep you safe. Can you do that?"

"I guess we'll find out," I sighed. My phone rang as his hands tightened in response to what I guessed was my less than satisfactory answer. Glancing down at my phone, I breathed a sigh of relief when I saw it was Mila calling me back. "I need to take this."

"We need to be careful about how many people know about your situation," he warned.

"It's my best friend calling me back," I explained. "And I'm not asking for your permission to talk to her. I'm telling you I'm taking this call."

"Feisty," he murmured before backing away.

"What in the world is going on with you?" Mila screeched in my ear as soon as the call connected. "Did you meet a mountain man hottie?"

"Not exactly," I answered. I told her about everything I'd learned since I got home, the words tumbling out quickly as she remained silent.

"Holy crap," she finally muttered. "Please tell me it's April Fools today. Or that your quirky sense of humor has run wild and this is all the plot of your next book."

"I wish I could, but I can't," I sighed just as Blaine walked back into the kitchen.

"We need to get going," he murmured into my ear.

"Is that him?" I barely registered Mila's question as shivers made their way up my spine from the feel of Blaine's hot breath against my skin. "Damn, he sounds as hot as he looks. Maybe you can squeeze in some time to clean out the cobwebs in your vagina while he's protecting you from the bad guys."

I couldn't hold back the snort of laughter her words caused. Unfortunately, she hadn't spoken quietly enough and Blaine's chuckle let me know he'd heard as well.

"Aren't you supposed to be worried about my safety?" I chided.

"I'm a woman. I'm good at multi-tasking." Her flippant response made me giggle.

"Love you," I whispered.

"Love you right back," she replied. "Let Mr. Hottie know if anything bad happens to you, he's going to answer to me."

"Will do."

"And if things get too crazy, have him bring you down here to me. We'll take the boat out and lose ourselves on the water for as long as it takes for this thing to blow over," she offered.

"Sounds like a plan," I agreed before hanging up, feeling less like I'd fallen down the rabbit hole after talking to Mila. It still felt like my entire world was spinning out of control, but the familiarity of hearing my best friend's voice was exactly what I needed to face what came next.

CHAPTER 5

Blaine

"Go pack a bag with whatever you'll need for the next few days," I instructed, pushing down my guilt at the shattered look in Delia's eyes and forcing myself to focus on the task at hand. She was a bigger distraction than she should be for a woman I'd just met, but it was difficult to ignore my reaction to her. Sending her up to her room to pack a bag served a double purpose since it also gave me some much-needed breathing room. Us, actually, since she wasn't immune to me either.

I'd caught the female awareness in her gaze a few times when she looked at me and I'd seen how my touch affected her. When I'd placed my hands on her shoulder, I had done so in an effort to offer comfort without any sexual intent. Then she'd shivered under my touch and it made me wonder how she'd react if I kissed her. If her phone hadn't rung right then, I wasn't positive I'd have been able to resist the temptation she presented. I'd never met a woman who had the ability to test my self-control the way she seemed to be able to do.

I knew it was wrong to let my thoughts wander in that direction, but I couldn't stop myself from imagining Delia moving beneath me as I thrust into her wet heat. Luckily, she was distracted by her phone call and I was able to get my cock under control by the time I walked back into the kitchen. She was already freaked out enough. The last thing I needed to do was make her think I was a sick pervert who wanted inside her panties—even though that's exactly what I felt like right about now.

I wasn't an active SEAL anymore, but I never forgot my training.

The mission.

The team.

The individual.

The mission always came first, followed by the team supporting the mission, and then the individuals who comprised the team. Finding out what happened to Serena was my mission, even if it was an unsanctioned one. I didn't answer to the Navy anymore, but I still answered to my own conscience.

Serena was part of my past, but she was still part of my team. Our connection hadn't ended just because our relationship had and we had lost touch. Only now, it looked like she had pulled Delia onto my team as well, if only while I cleaned up this mess, which meant I couldn't afford to think of Delia as an individual—or a highly desirable woman.

It had been a long time since I'd been involved with a woman, but that never interfered with my ability to focus in the past. There were times when we were overseas when I'd gone without sex for a helluva lot longer than it had been for me now. It hadn't gotten to me back then and I couldn't let it get to me now. Delia was just another part of this mission.

Soft footfalls on the carpeted stairs had me looking up. A couple moments later, Delia walked back into the kitchen. Even rumpled from our earlier struggle, she managed to look sexy. Knowing she could pack a bag faster than some sailors made her even hotter. Most of the women I knew would have taken at least an hour to pick out what to pack and then they would have spent the next thirty minutes or so fixing their hair and makeup because they wouldn't want a man to see them as anything less than perfectly put together. Knowing what I saw was what I got with Delia made her all the more attractive. Shaking my head, I shoved the thought aside and walked to the sliding glass door to retrieve my go bag.

"We'll need to take your car. If the police come back and find it in the garage when it wasn't here earlier, it would raise red flags," I explained as I moved to the front windows and glanced outside, making sure there wasn't anyone who would see us leave.

"What about your car? If the police talked to my neighbors and they noticed a strange car in the neighborhood, wouldn't they call it in?" she asked, coming up behind me, her eyes darting around nervously as she looked out the window. "Or what if they saw me when I got home?"

I reached for her bag with my free hand and gestured for her to lead the way into the garage. "A cab dropped me off and either they didn't see you or they thought it was a family member. If they'd called it in, the police would have been here by now."

"I guess that's a lucky thing," she mumbled as I shifted her bag into the hand that held my go bag so I could help her into the passenger seat.

I walked around to the other side of the car and tossed the bags in the backseat before climbing into the driver's seat. Smiling to myself at the irritated sound she made as she handed over the keys, I started the engine but kept the lights off as I waited for the garage door to open. Watching the darkened street behind me, I quickly backed out of her drive and got us down the street as fast as possible without squealing the tires.

"Did you learn to drive in the dark and break into houses while you were a SEAL?" Delia asked, shifting in her seat so she was facing me.

"Yeah," I answered, hoping the one-word answer made it clear to her that I wasn't interested in conversation.

Unfortunately, she didn't catch my hint or she just didn't care because she kept asking questions. "Why?"

The answer I'd heard my Colonel give enough times over the years that it was now drilled into my head popped out of my mouth. "Y is a crooked letter. Nobody ever got it straight."

I hadn't intended to make her giggle, but damn if I could be unhappy to hear the sound even if I was trying like hell to distance myself from her. "You're from Vegas?"

"I live there now."

She snorted. "I'm getting the impression you only want me to talk when necessary. Wouldn't you rather things be a little friendlier than that? We're going to be together for the next several days, don't you think it would be a whole lot easier if we found a way to get along well enough so things aren't awkward between us?"

"Fine, ask away," I offered.

"How old are you?"

"My birthdate was on my driver's license."

"Darn it, I didn't even think to look," she mumbled as she pulled her phone out of her purse and peered at the screen. "Twenty-seven. I would have guessed at least thirty."

Fucking A, had she just told me I looked old? "Is that supposed to be an insult?"

"Oh, please! Like you don't know how hot you look. I'm sure women all around the world fall all over themselves around you," she scoffed. "Don't even try to act offended because I thought you looked older than you really are. It's the way you hold yourself. You have the confidence of someone older and don't seem as immature as most of the twenty-something guys I've met."

"The military will do that to you."

"I guess that makes sense," she sighed. "Are your parents proud of your military service?"

I hesitated a moment and then surprised myself by answering. "I like to think so, but it's complicated. My dad died when I was little, leaving my mom to raise me on her own. They were high school sweethearts. Married young. Had me not too long after he finished basic training. The irony is he wasn't going to re-up when his contract was over. He was all set to move to the IRR so he wouldn't miss out on more of my childhood. Instead, he came home to us in a body bag."

"It must have been hard for your mom when you enlisted."

"She wasn't thrilled, but she understood my decision." To deflect the conversation away from myself, I lobbed the question back to her. "What about your parents? Are they proud of your writing career?"

"I'm not sure proud is the right word exactly," she giggled. "They're happy about my success but also a little embarrassed I write romance. They had me when they were older, almost in their forties. My mom titters about it with her friends and my dad likes to pretend my books don't have any sex in them."

Hearing the word sex from her lips had my cock twitching in my jeans. I'd never read a romance novel in my life, but knowing she wrote sex scenes had me wanting to crack one of her books open so I could read one of them—maybe get a glimpse into some of her fantasies. Some of her desires. "Maybe I'll have to give them a try sometime."

"Pervert," she muttered, looking out the window. She finally fell silent just as she managed to catch my undivided attention. The conversation had served its purpose, though. The silence between us was devoid of the awkwardness that had been there initially. It had been replaced with an entirely different tension now— the sexual kind.

Thirty minutes into the drive, I was kicking myself for not sleeping more while I was on the plane last night. I knew better than that and should have grabbed as much sleep as I could while it was available. Now the rhythmic motion of the tires was making me drowsy. Luckily, we didn't have much further to go.

I tightened my grip on the steering wheel and glanced in the rearview mirror again. As far as I could tell, we weren't being followed, which made me breathe a little easier. When we made it to Damian's crash pad in the city, my first priority was reviewing all the information Brody had gathered. I fucking hated operating in the dark. It was no way to run a mission, even if it was off-book. I needed to figure out what the fuck had happened to Serena and what kind of shit-storm she'd landed Delia and I smack dab in the middle of.

****

Less than ten minutes later, the door to a penthouse suite in a boutique hotel was closing behind me— courtesy of my boss. Delia's shocked reaction to our surroundings had me glancing around, trying to see it through her eyes. It wasn't the type of hotel room most people ever laid eyes on and something I would have been impressed with had I not spent the last year surrounded by even more luxurious surroundings. A big-screen television rested front and center, directly opposite from a black leather couch and matching recliner. A dark grey throw rug covered a large portion of the hardwood floor with a glass-topped coffee table placed in the middle. There was a full kitchen to the left, complete with granite countertops and stainless steel appliances. I saw a king sized bed through the door to the right. Another sweep of the room confirmed it was the only bed available.

"Take the bed. You need to sleep," I said as I walked into the bedroom and laid her bag on the plush comforter.

She had followed me into the room but raised an eyebrow at the order. "You're a lot bigger than I am, frogman. I think it would be better if I took the couch and you took the bed."

"I've slept in worse places," I argued. "And it's going to be a while before I'll be getting any sleep tonight."

I watched her hand as it moved over the dark grey comforter, lightly tracing the cream-colored, horizontal stripes. "The bed's certainly large enough for two and I've been told I'm a sound sleeper."

Her hint wasn't subtle. An image of the two of us entwined together on the bed's surface flashed through my brain. I was sure she was making the offer out of kindness, wanting to make sure I got a good night's sleep. Her life as she had known it this morning had been shot to hell. She was in an unknown place, trusting her life to me—a man she had met hours ago when I'd manhandled her after breaking into her home. Yet, here she was, more concerned about my comfort than her own.

Damn, she was sweet. Too sweet for her own good. A less honorable man wouldn't hesitate before taking advantage of her softness. She was the kind of woman men dreamed about when they served their country. The reward we hoped to have earned by the time we came back home. And here she was, standing in front of me, offering to share the only available bed—ripe for the plucking.

"How about you get your pretty little ass in that bed before you fall over and we'll see where I end up sleeping once I'm done?"

"Pretty. Little. Ass?" she gasped.

She was too damn cute to pull off the outraged look she was most likely aiming for. Even if she had managed it, there was a hint of satisfaction in her gaze giving her away. She definitely liked me thinking of her ass. And based on the heated blush rising up her neck, it was entirely possible she didn't mind my domineering tone either. It was yet another quality about her that made her damn near irresistible.

"Bed," I growled, turning on my heel and striding quickly from the room before I succumbed to temptation and threw her, and myself, onto the bed.

Gripping the knob in my fist, I shut the door firmly behind me—not slamming it, but using enough force to make Delia think twice before she decided to do something stupid like follow after me. I stood still on the other side of the door, my heart beating wildly as I listened to her muttering before the slamming of the bathroom door let me know she was getting ready for bed. I breathed a sigh of relief before grabbing my go bag and settling in on the couch. I called Brody for a status update as I fired my computer up and connected it to the hotel's Wi-Fi, pulling up my email so I could see what he'd already sent me.

"Things have been so damn quiet since we got out, I'd started wishing for trouble just so I could feel alive again. You ever hear me do something as batshit crazy as that again, promise me you'll kick my sorry ass until I'm thinking straight," he said before I could even say hello. He sounded more rattled than when he'd woken up in the hospital bed after our last mission.

"What you found, it's that bad?"

"Shit, no. Sorry," he apologized. "I haven't been able to figure out the thing with Serena yet. I sent you the background information I gathered on her, her boyfriend, and Delia Sinclair. Serena looks fairly clean, except she lives a much nicer lifestyle than her job should afford her. One that appears to be paid for by the boyfriend, but I haven't been able to trace the source of his wealth yet. No criminal file on him, but there's something about him that seems off. I need to do some more digging there."

"And Delia?"

"Clean as a whistle. She doesn't even have a parking ticket. Pays her bills on time, owns her house free and clear. I even found a purchase for a second home she put in her parent's name. All the deposits into her account can be traced back to royalties. Not a single sign of anything fishy." His words confirmed my impression of Delia and my shoulders sagged in relief. "Seriously, Saint. I don't think I've ever run a check on someone that's come up this clean before. She could steal your nickname if she wanted it, that's how lily white she is. She sure as hell didn't deserve to be dragged into this mess by Serena."

"Tell me something I don't already know," I muttered, once again feeling the weight of the guilt for how I might have to use Delia. She was an innocent, but her striking resemblance to Serena could come in handy down the line. "If I'd been here sooner, Serena would have had other options. Delia would have been clear of the situation and there wouldn't be a body lying in the morgue right now. One we both know is almost definitely Serena."

"Or there could have been two bodies and I'd be on my way into town to avenge your death," he argued.

"Killing a defenseless woman is a helluva lot different than taking down a SEAL. If I'd been here, odds are they wouldn't have been able to touch her."

"Except we don't even know who *they* are," Brody retorted. "I know you have to be torn up inside about Serena, but you need to remind yourself that you weren't the one who got her into this mess. She's the one who pulled you and an innocent woman into it and didn't even leave you any clues to help you find a way out of it."

"And we only have four days to get to the bottom of this before Delia is going to insist on calling in the cops," I said before filling him in on the details of my conversation with Delia. "We've got our work cut out for us."

"The only easy day was yesterday," Brody reminded me. He'd always been good at putting things into perspective like that. It was something he'd been doing since the day we met.

"And every day is a battle," I agreed.

"Some battles are harder than others, my brother. When they're personal, it makes it that much more difficult. Hell, just ask Prez. You wouldn't believe the shit that went down with Kade. He and D are down in Florida trying to pull his ass out of prison."

We'd met Prez, Kade, and D during hell week. They were an interesting trio who had formed a friendship as tight as mine with Brody, one which had strengthened over time as they served on a team together. I'd heard enough stories about Kade to know he'd been a bit of a hothead when he'd joined the Navy, but by the time I'd met him, he'd mellowed out and was on the straight and narrow. "Prison?"

"Some dumb-fuck jury down in Florida found him guilty of murder."

The last I'd heard anything about Kade, he was heading home on a leave of absence because his grandfather, who had raised him, and younger brother were ill. Brody and I were getting ready to head overseas on a mission—our final one. When we'd made it stateside again, we'd had to deal with surgery and rehabilitation plus the news that we'd never be able to serve on a SEAL team again. "When the hell did this happen? Why didn't we hear about it?"

"The murder happened while we were radio silent. Kade's grandfather needed him home so he didn't re-up. Got into trouble his first day home. The trial just ended a little more than six months ago. I'm not sure why we hadn't heard the news before this, but he hadn't been able to get word to Prez and D until now because their mission had been extended. They need some help hacking some company down there and reached out to me last night."

"And the hits just keep coming." It was a tough position to be in, knowing I needed Brody's expertise to find out what happened to Serena just as much as Kade needed him to clear his name. "I hope you stocked up on those disgusting energy drinks you love so much. It looks like your skills are in high demand."

"Aren't they always," he joked.

"Seriously, man. If you need to pull off this to help out Kade, I'll understand. I don't like the idea of him living in a square box, paying for a crime we both know he didn't commit."

It wasn't that I couldn't believe another SEAL would take a man's life. With the right motivation, he absolutely would. He would just be smart enough to make sure he didn't get caught doing it—and sure as shit not on his first day home after he left a career he loved to take care of a dying family member.

"No way am I going to leave you swinging in the wind, Saint," he argued. "And you seriously underestimate my skills if you don't think I'll be able to handle your thing and crack Consolidated's system without breaking a sweat."

"Just do me a favor and don't get caught. The last thing I need right now is your brother breathing down my neck because I helped you put your ass in a sling," I grumbled.

"What big brother doesn't know won't hurt him."

I laughed at how blind Brody was about Damian sometimes. "You're bullshitting yourself if you don't think he knows exactly what type of shit you're up to even when he's out of town. Your brother might not be a SEAL, but he would have made one hell of a General."

"You looking to trade up in the best friend department?"

"I don't know," I sighed. "Your brother was nice enough to lend me a safe place to stay. Good security, suite on the top floor. Although, it's only a one bedroom, so I might have to bust his balls about that."

Brody's whistle was shrill, even filtered through the phone line. "Only one bed, huh? You shacking up with an angel on a mission, Saint?"

"Fuck you."

"I don't know, man. I saw her picture and I'm pretty sure you'd much rather be fucking her instead. She looks like she'd be fun in the sack with all those curves."

Talking shit about women, even ones we'd banged, wasn't unusual for us. When you'd been through hell together, nothing was really off limits. But hearing Brody talk about Delia that way had me seeing red in an instant. "Don't ever talk about her like that again, Hack."

"Holy fucking shit," he whispered. "Alrighty then. I think I'll avoid that topic like the plague. But I'll keep you updated when I get more to go on. My guess is when you're done reading the reports I sent over, you'll come to the same conclusion I did."

"And what was that?"

"You gotta find a way to question Serena's co-workers and see if she was acting weird."

I scanned through the report on Serena and found the name of her employer. "Any sign she was close with anyone there?"

"Nothing in her email or phone records. Looks like she went out to lunch to a Mexican restaurant down the street from work pretty regularly. Receipts show food and drinks for two a few times, so maybe you'll get lucky during your visit and find someone who knows what was going on in her life before she disappeared."

"Thank fuck," I breathed. Finally, I had a lead to follow. It might be a slim one, but it was more than I'd had all day. "I'll recon her place of employment tomorrow and find a way in."

"I'm sure you will. Send me a text with anything you need me to follow-up. And if it's anything urgent, call me. I'm sure I'll be up late tonight getting what Prez needs on Consolidated for Kane."

I settled into the couch, making myself comfortable as I read through all the information Brody had managed to pull together. Once I made it through it all, I couldn't help but think, once again, the man was a genius behind the keyboard. *I have no doubt he'll do exactly what he said he would*, I thought as my eyes drifted shut.

CHAPTER 6

Delia

When I'd climbed into bed last night, I was certain I'd never be able to fall asleep. My mind was racing with thoughts about Serena and what might have happened to her, the news story announcing to the world that I'd been murdered, and the breathtakingly hot man who might have climbed into bed with me at any moment. I shouldn't have been able to roll over and drift off to sleep like I didn't have a care in the world, but as I opened bleary eyes to a room lit by the sun streaming in through the blinds, I realized that's exactly what I'd done.

A quick glance at the other side of the bed confirmed my suspicion—Blaine hadn't slept with me. I wasn't certain whether I should have been relieved or offended, but I still couldn't believe I'd actually had the nerve to suggest sharing in the first place. If I was going to worry about anything, it should have been the fact that Blaine had the power to make me do things I normally wouldn't consider.

As though I conjured him from my thoughts, he was the first thing I saw as I stumbled into the living room. I wasn't prepared for the sight of him sitting on the couch, pieces of a gun sitting on the table as he appeared to be cleaning it. It wasn't the gun that startled me—he was a former Navy SEAL, after all—it was seeing him shirtless for the first time. Muscles bunched and rippled with each movement and the surge of desire I felt at seeing his bare chest was so strong, it almost brought me to my knees. It wasn't like I hadn't seen attractive men before. Heck, I'd slept with a guy who, at the time, I thought was hot enough to be a model. But nobody held a candle to Blaine's sheer masculinity. He was most definitely not a pretty boy. He was *all* man—the kind who made me happy to be a woman.

When his piercing blue eyes locked with mine, I fiddled with my hair nervously, wishing I'd taken the time to make myself look more presentable before rolling out of bed in search of coffee. His gaze swept down, making me acutely aware of the thin material of my camisole as my nipples puckered in reaction to his lingering look. I crossed my arms in front of my body protectively, and just about groaned when I realized the movement pushed my boobs up even higher. The smirk on Blaine's face made it clear he knew he was the reason I was uncomfortable—and he took enjoyment in that knowledge.

"Morning," I mumbled grumpily, frowning as he reached over and grabbed a shirt to put on.

"Get a good night's sleep?" he asked.

"Yeah," I whispered, pulling my gaze from the strip of skin showing when he unbuttoned his jeans to tuck in his shirt.

The strength of my attraction to him unsettled me. I'd only met him last night and under the strangest of circumstances. He shouldn't have been able to scatter my senses so easily, no matter how hot he was. It just didn't make sense. Yet, here I was, mentally removing that shirt right off his chest and taking his jeans along with it.

"How are you feeling?"

I stared at him blankly for a moment, finding it difficult to concentrate on his words while my mind was busy undressing him and picturing several things I'd take great satisfaction in doing to his muscular body.

"Hmm?" I murmured.

"You're looking steadier on your feet than you were last night. Feeling better?" he asked as he stood up and walked toward me. I dropped my eyes to the ground in an effort not to get sucked into his compelling gaze and noticed his feet were bare. I hated feet, yet there was something intimate about seeing our naked feet so close to each other once he was standing in front of me.

"Yeah, I must have been more tired than I thought. I slept like a baby," I mumbled.

"You hungry?"

The thought of food had my stomach growling and I flushed in embarrassment. "I'm starving."

"How about I make you breakfast?"

"You cook?" I asked, surprised by the offer.

"It's a skill my mom made sure I had, and I'm damn glad she did. I like to eat, so it comes in handy."

"I'm sure it does." Most of the guys I knew couldn't even boil a pot of water. It was nice to meet one who could actually cook and offered to do so. "Like right now when I'd kill for some food."

"How about we leave the potential killing to me?"

Glancing at the gun on the table, I couldn't help the shiver racing up my spine at the thought that he had probably killed people in the line of duty. "That works for me."

"C'mon then," he said, holding his hand out for mine. He led me into the kitchenette and helped me onto one of the stools at the counter. "I checked earlier and it looks like we have everything I need to make a couple omelets."

"Sounds good."

I placed my elbows on the countertop and leaned my head against an open palm, watching him pull eggs, ham, cheese, and a tomato out of the refrigerator. Then he opened the cupboards in search of a frying pan and mixing bowl. "Romance novels?"

I hesitated before answering. Explaining my career to guys had gone wrong too many times in the past. I'd quickly discovered a lot of men were either intimidated by the idea that I wrote steaming hot sex or they assumed it meant I'd be ready to hop into bed with them at the drop of a hat. "Yeah. I've always enjoyed reading romance and was shocked when an agent snapped up my first book and managed to sell it to a publisher."

"How long ago was that?" he asked as he started to break open a half dozen eggs.

"About four years ago."

"You were what, twenty back then?" I raised my eyebrows at him, surprised he knew my age. He grimaced a little before telling me something I already should have thought of myself. "I had Brody run a background check on you."

"Can you let him know I'm sorry for almost putting him to sleep?" I joked, appalled to think about how boring they both must have found it. My life was incredibly dull—especially compared to two ex-Navy SEALs.

"I also searched your house before you got there," he admitted softly.

"Oh my God," I groaned, letting my head drop onto the counter. On the surface, I kept my home decently clean, though I was pretty sure his idea of a search wasn't wandering from room to room without looking in closets or drawers. Or under the beds. "Please, just kill me now."

"Hey," he said softly, moving around the counter to rub my back gently. "Don't be embarrassed."

"Can we just tattoo the word 'slob' on my forehead and get it over with?"

I lifted my head when he chuckled. "Trust me, I've seen worse. Much, much worse."

"I'm a bit of a hoarder," I admitted. "An absent-minded one."

"An adorable one," he corrected, running a finger along my cheek before heading back to stir the eggs.

"Yeah, adorable," I repeated grumpily, not exactly thrilled that the guy who made me drool thought I was something as mundane as adorable. I preferred him to think of me as sexy or irresistible.

"And an incredibly talented one if you managed to sign a publishing deal when you were twenty." Blaine flashed a grin at me as he poured the egg mixture into the hot pan.

The admiration in his tone helped to soothe my hurt feelings. "There's a lot of luck involved, too. So many authors out there are way more talented than me. I was just in the right place at the right time with the right story."

"Don't sell yourself short, Delia. You wouldn't have done half as well if you didn't have a gift."

I smiled at the snap in his tone. "I think it's hard for me to think of it that way since I've always been an avid reader. It's a little surreal to think of myself in the same light as authors whose books I've read over and over again."

He turned to look at me. "I hope you figure out a way to start." His eyes met mine, but before I could reply, he turned back to the eggs, sprinkling the rest of the ingredients into the frying pan. "I'm sure you've been asked this a million times before..."

I cringed and braced myself, waiting for the inevitable dirty comment about sex scenes and feeling acute disappointment at the idea of him ruining what had been a lovely conversation.

"But how do you manage to come up with so many different story ideas?"

The spurt of amazed laughter spilling from my lips was as much of a surprise as his question had been— but a pleasant one. "I find inspiration in all sorts of places," I answered, thinking he certainly offered a wealth of it. "People watching, stories I've heard, newspaper articles, personal experiences, dreams. Some of my best ideas have come to me in a flash in the middle of the night. Luckily, I keep a notepad next to the bed so I don't forget them all when I wake up. Or in the shower, but it's a little more tricky to jot stuff down when I'm wet."

By the time I finished my answer, Blaine was sliding the omelet onto a plate, along with some toast. "Never thought I'd hear a woman complain about not being able to take notes when she's wet." The devilish glint in his eye and tilt of his lips made me a little weak in the knees. "Maybe you need a volunteer, someone to help you dry off when that happens."

I could think of a lot of other things he could help with in the shower and none of them involved a towel or drying off—more like getting dirty and wet at the same time. "Maybe I do," I finally answered.

"Coffee, juice, or milk?" he offered.

"Coffee, please."

He grabbed a mug from the cupboard and filled it for me. "How do you take it?"

"Black."

The smile he flashed me was filled with approval as he split the omelet in half and moved it onto a second plate, adding toast to that one as well. He set one of the plates in front of me and slid onto the stool next to me. My stomach growled again, reminding me it had been too many hours since my last meal. I took a bite of the omelet and nodded in appreciation.

I only made it about halfway through my plate before I was full. Blaine was still eating and I forced my gaze away from him to survey my surroundings. When my eyes roamed the living room, I noticed the throw blanket stuffed into a corner and the laptop on the floor. "Did you manage to get any sleep at all?"

"Enough to get me by," he replied.

When he finished his meal, I got up and gathered the dirty dishes to rinse them off in the sink. "Something you learned as a SEAL?"

"Yes and no. My mom would be the first to tell you I didn't sleep much as a kid. Always had too much energy to burn. It was useful when the only sleep I could grab was a combat nap here and there, so I can't really complain anymore when she razzes me about it."

"It looks like you were busy last night. Have you figured out what you're going to do?"

"Without any word from Serena yet, I have to move forward with the assumption that she used your name to check into the hotel and they somehow found her and killed her. Brody's working on confirming the identity of the body in the morgue. As long as they upload whatever data they've already collected, he'll be able to get his hands on it." He looked pensive, reminding me he knew Serena well enough for her to call him for help when she was in danger.

"You never did tell me how you knew Serena." I wasn't sure why, but he looked uncomfortable with my question.

"We grew up together. Our moms are close friends."

"Oh," I sighed. Now I was the one who felt uncomfortable. A woman he'd known since he was a kid might have been murdered a day ago and here I was asking pesky questions about her.

His hand rubbed the back of his neck as he stared at the floor. "I haven't seen her in years, but we also dated back in high school."

That explained his discomfort. The sparks had been flying between us and we had only met because his ex-girlfriend resembled me closely enough to pass as my sister—and she might be dead. It certainly was an awkward situation. One that warranted a change of topic.

"What are we going to be doing while Brody is busy hacking into police records?"

"*I'm* going to work on identifying and locating the unsubs."

Crossing my arms over my chest, I raised my eyebrow to express my displeasure with his response. He was making it crystal clear he didn't want me to get involved, and he managed to do it in one short sentence. "And while you're doing that, I'm going to be sitting here twiddling my thumbs?"

"If that's what it takes to keep you safe."

If we were cartoon characters, steam would be coming out of my ears. "How are you going to find the bad guys?"

"Brody sent me the address for Serena's work. I'll head over there and ask a few questions. See if she has a co-worker who knows what was going on with her."

"Where did she work?"

"A real estate office downtown. Not too far from her townhouse."

I didn't have a lot of experience with co-workers since my first novel had been picked up while I was

78

still in college, but I knew women well enough to know they weren't likely to share personal information about a friend with some strange guy—even if he was hot. Not without a compelling reason to spill, anyway. And I didn't like the jealousy that flared when I concluded he'd only be able to get one of them to talk by flirting. "Take a good look at me, Blaine."

I shivered as his eyes locked with mine. "I already have every inch of you memorized."

"It would be so much easier if you took me with you," I urged. "We could say I'm Serena's sister and I'm worried about her because I haven't been able to reach her but it hasn't been long enough for the police to let me file a missing persons report."

"Saying you're her sister is too risky. If someone there knows her well enough to know what she'd gotten into, then odds are they'll also know she's an only child."

I wanted to stomp my foot in frustration at the logic behind his statement, but I resisted. In the end, I knew it wouldn't help me convince him that I could be an asset and not a liability. "Then I'll be her cousin. We look enough alike that nobody would question it and it's not likely anyone there knows her entire family tree."

"I'd feel better if you stayed behind. I don't have the slightest clue what happened to Serena yet. For all I know, it could be connected to her work."

I broke out the big guns and gave him the puppy dog eyes, batting my eyelashes for good measure. "It's a real estate office in a crowded city. How much trouble could I possibly get into when you're there with me?"

"Shit," he mumbled.

"Please take me with you," I pleaded, pushing harder since I could tell he was actually considering it. The last thing I wanted was to get stuck all alone for the day in this suite, no matter how luxurious it was. I'd just spent ten days by myself. I didn't want to spend the next four the same way. Definitely not when I could be with Blaine instead.

"If you come with me, then you need to stick close to me. Listen to what I say. Do what I say when I say to do it. Do you think you can do that?"

"Absolutely," I agreed, practically bouncing on the balls of my feet in excitement.

"This isn't a field trip. It's a reconnaissance mission. We get in, get the intel we need, and get out."

"In and out," I repeated. "Understood."

Blaine wrapped his hands around my arms as he looked down at me. "Using your cover story makes sense."

"It does." My heart leaped in excitement. I tried to dampen my enthusiasm, wanting to project an air of confidence, not giddiness.

"But we have to use it today. Once we get past the forty-eight-hour mark, we won't have an excuse for not bringing the police into it."

"I can be ready to go whenever you need me to be," I offered.

He shook his head slightly. "I can't believe I'm actually going to do this," he mumbled before his voice firmed with determination. "Be ready in thirty minutes. Dress comfortably—no skirts, no heels. If I tell you to run, you need to be able to move fast."

"I packed gym shoes and jeans."

"Go. Before I change my mind."

"Thank you," I whispered, rising on my toes to place my lips lightly over his in gratitude, as if it kissing him was the most natural thing in the world for me to do. I only had my surprise to blame since being that bold was so out of character for me. When what I had just done registered in my brain, I started to pull away so I could apologize. I didn't get far, though. One of Blaine's hands slid up my arm and over my neck, holding me in place.

CHAPTER 7

Blaine

Cupping the back of Delia's neck, I pulled her closer to my body. With the most innocent of gestures, she already had my heart racing and my cock hard and aching. As much as I wanted to ravage her mouth, her startled gasp before she tried to step away from me let me know she wasn't ready for me to deepen the kiss. So I kept the connection between us gentle, lowering my lips and softly brushing them against hers. I ran my tongue across her bottom lip before taking it into my mouth and nipping at it—wanting her to open for me. On another gasp, her lips parted and my tongue dipped inside, tangling with hers. I allowed myself to savor the taste of her for a moment before easing away.

I had to bite back a groan as I watched Delia's tongue swipe across her lower lip, capturing the taste of my kiss. Her eyes were glazed, lids lowered halfway. The pulse in her neck was fluttering and her hands were clenched, my shirt bunched in them. I felt great satisfaction in knowing she felt the same pull between us.

"I've never felt anything like this before." I'd been on missions involving women, but I'd never been tempted to cross the line with any of them. With Delia, it was like the line had been obliterated.

"Neither have I," she admitted.

I was relieved to know I wasn't in this alone, but the timing of our meeting sucked. "We can't do this now. Not when I need to concentrate on figuring out what happened to Serena and keeping you safe."

The mood between us shifted at my words—a heady reminder that a girl who used to mean a lot to me was most likely dead. She wasn't just the girl next door growing up, Serena had been the last woman I'd called my girlfriend, even though she was just a girl back then. After we had broken up, I had way too much fun fucking my way through the rest of high school to bother with another relationship. I'd been a teenage boy with more than enough responsibility on my shoulders. I wasn't about to voluntarily add another one to my plate, not when girls were more than willing to give it up without a commitment.

The situation didn't change any when I joined the Navy, especially once I earned my budweiser. If I was horny, it was damn easy to go out and find someone for the night, maybe a weekend, if I was coming off a particularly hard mission. My hook-ups never lasted more than a week and I'd been comfortable with the way things were. Then my life was shot to hell along with my knee and a night of hard fucking with a stranger didn't hold the same appeal.

I hadn't planned for a long dry spell, but that's what ended up happening anyway. At first, it was because I was going through rehab for my knee. Once I'd healed up, finding pussy should have been the first thing I did, but I was too busy trying to wrap my head around not being a SEAL anymore to bother with it. Then Damian offered me a lifeline and I focused all my attention on whipping his security team into shape—in Vegas, where hot women looking for a good time surrounded me.

Somehow, I still hadn't managed to break my dry spell, and fuck it all if Delia wasn't the first woman in years to capture my attention enough for me to think I might want more than a fuck or two. She did more than just get my dick hard and it was beyond fucked up to think I only met her because Serena was in trouble. The reminder felt like a bucket of cold water on my libido, allowing me to refocus my energy on the task at hand.

Forcing myself to remove my hands from Delia's body was harder than it should have been, which would have worried me had I given myself time to think about it. "You have twenty-five minutes left."

My words were harsh considering the kiss we just shared, deliberately so in an effort to create some distance. Based on the stiffening of Delia's body and the wounded look in her eyes before she turned away, they had the desired effect. It surprised me how much her hurt feelings affected me, but I still let her go without softening the blow. I wasn't a soft man and now was as good a time as any for her to realize what she was getting into with me if we became involved— even though I knew it was a dick move.

****

Less than thirty minutes later, Delia and I were in her car headed to Serena's office. She had taken my instructions to heart, dressing exactly as I requested. She even managed to get ready with five minutes to spare and damn near beat me to the door. What was even more impressive was the silent treatment she gave me during the drive. In my experience, women liked to talk everything to death. It didn't matter whether they were a one night stand, a wife of one of the guys on the team, or my mom—if you hurt a woman's feelings, you were going to hear about it.

I should have been happy with the silence, but Delia's way of handling it was effective. I found myself wanting her to talk to me. About her feelings. *And didn't that just make me sound like a pussy?*

I let the silence stand and felt a sizzle of awareness each time her eyes slid my way. It happened often and I took satisfaction in watching as her frustration with my lack of reaction grew. When she started tapping her foot and shifting in her seat, I had a feeling she was barely holding her temper in check. With every huff of breath she made, the tension between us grew until the air was practically crackling. Patience was a virtue BUD/S training had drilled into me. A tool I yielded with expert precision in my battle of wills against Delia—I had no intention of losing. When she finally cracked, I turned my head away from her so she couldn't see my smile.

"One day. That's all it took." Her voice was a light rasp, sounding as if the words were being torn from her. "I met you less than twenty-four hours ago and in that short time you've broken into my home, manhandled me, told me I was presumed murdered, convinced me not to call the police, carted me off to a luxurious suite for the night, didn't share the bed with me when I offered, made me an amazing breakfast, kissed me senseless, and managed to piss me off more than any man before you has ever done."

When she listed it all out like that, I had to admit, I'd put her through a lot. It didn't mean I was going to bend, though. "Actually, I broke into your home before you met me."

"Argh," she growled.

"And I wouldn't call it manhandling. I neutralized you as a threat until I could get you to calm down, but I did it gently. You and I both know I could have hurt you had that been my intention."

"I suppose you're right about that," she begrudgingly admitted, her pretty lips twisted into a pout.

"I can't deny convincing you not to call the police, but it was for the greater good. I guess I could switch us to somewhere less comfortable if you'd prefer not to go back to the suite. And I promise to make your food taste crappy next time I cook for you, if that'll make you happy."

"Who says I'm going to let you cook for me again after you were such an ass earlier?"

I had skipped several of her points on purpose, but there she was, striking right at the heart of the matter. She wasn't going to let me get away with the bullshit I'd pulled earlier. I was beginning to think there was more to Delia Sinclair than met the eye, and there was already a hell of a lot I liked about what my eyes could see.

I waited to respond until I pulled the car into a spot in the lot next to Serena's office. Leaving the engine running, I turned to Delia. "I slept fine on the couch."

"And?"

"If I'd joined you in that bed, I don't know that I'd be able to say the same thing." Until I saw her eyes flash with relief, I hadn't considered she might have thought I slept on the couch because I wasn't interested in her. "But as much as I know I shouldn't have kissed you this morning, I don't regret it."

"Then why?"

"Because it needed to be done," I said, turning off the engine and exiting the car. It was an effective way to end the conversation without really answering her question—not in the way I figured she wanted it to be answered, at least. The glare she leveled at me said she wasn't happy, but she followed me into the office anyway.

"Welcome to Westhampton Realty," a pretty, dark-haired woman greeted us. "How can I help you?"

I wasn't sure how effective Delia would be at lying, so I took the lead. "My girlfriend was hoping her cousin Serena was working today."

"Serena Taylor?" the woman asked. When her gaze shifted toward Delia, her eyes rounded in surprise. "Wow! You and Serena could pass as sisters."

"We hear that whenever we're together," Delia replied.

"I'm sorry, but she isn't in the office today. She left a voicemail asking for some time off a couple days ago. I thought she said it was for a family emergency, but maybe I misunderstood since you'd know if that were the case, being her cousin and all."

"That's why we're trying so hard to find her," I explained. "Nobody has been able to reach her. She's not at home and she isn't answering her phone. We were hoping one of her co-workers would know where she was since it's unlike Serena to disappear like this, especially during a family crisis."

The receptionist looked over her shoulder toward a blonde woman talking on the phone. "She and Tasha are pretty close. I was just getting ready to leave for an early lunch, but you could wait until she's done with her call to talk to her if you'd like."

I switched my gaze to Delia. "That sound good to you, baby?"

"I don't know what else we can do." Her voice quavered and the receptionist made a sympathetic noise before moving toward Tasha's desk with a note.

I wrapped my arm around Delia's shoulder, projecting an air of concern as I led her to a chair. "Everything's going to be okay. We'll figure out what's going on with Serena."

The receptionist stopped by our chairs before leaving. "I let Tasha know you're waiting. It sounded like she was wrapping up her call so it shouldn't be too much longer."

"Thank you," Delia whispered.

"You're welcome, honey," she replied, reaching a hand out to pat Delia's shoulder. "Wish I could've been more help. Serena's a sweetie."

She walked out the door and about a minute later, the blonde realtor walked toward us. "Hi, I'm Tasha. You're looking for Serena?"

"Nice to meet you, Tasha." I stood and held my hand out to shake hers. "I'm Blaine and this is my girlfriend, Delia. Serena's her cousin and we're worried about her. No one has been able to reach her. We were hoping you might have an idea of where we could look or someone we could call...anything we might not have thought of already."

"Missing?" Tasha gasped. "But I just talked to her a couple days ago."

"The last time any of us were able to reach her was a little more than twenty-four hours ago," I explained. "We've tried calling her cell, stopping by her house. Her mom hasn't heard from her."

"What about Jonathan?" Tasha asked.

"We haven't been able to reach him. My aunt and I don't have his number. Is there any chance you might have it?" Delia's expression was a mixture of hope and worry. She was doing better at maintaining our cover than I could have hoped, drawing both of the women into her act and making them want to help her.

"I do." Tasha walked back to her desk and grabbed her cell phone. She fiddled with it for a minute before rattling off a number while I jotted it down.

"Has she seemed okay lately? I've been so busy, I haven't spoken to her as often as I should. I hate that I'm so out of touch with what's going on in her life. I feel horrible about not realizing sooner when I might have been able to do something to help her before she disappeared like this," Delia said.

"No, don't talk that way. Don't even feel that way," Tasha chided. "Even if you hadn't drifted apart, I don't think she would have told you what was wrong."

"But I'll never know unless I find her."

Tasha shook her head. "She's my friend and I see her just about every day, but she didn't tell me anything."

"No problems at work?" I asked, trying to keep the conversation on point. We needed information and this woman was our best shot at getting it—even if she didn't think she had anything for us.

"Not that I'm aware of, and I'd be the first person she'd tell since we gossip about work all the time."

The report Brody sent on Jonathan Roberts left me with more questions than answers. "Boyfriend trouble?"

Her pause was answer enough. I nudged Delia's foot, wanting her to push the issue. Odds were good Tasha would be more receptive to talk about Serena's relationship with another woman. Luckily, she took the hint.

"I know you're Serena's friend and it probably doesn't feel right talking about her like this, but if there's anything you can think of—anything at all—it might help. The police won't let us file a missing person's report until tomorrow, but I *know* something's wrong. She wouldn't disappear like this. Especially not when her mom is sick," Delia pleaded with her.

Tasha's eyes flickered and her throat worked before she spoke. "She seemed a little off when we went to lunch on Monday."

"Off?" Delia repeated.

She glanced over her shoulder to make sure nobody was nearby before continuing in a low voice. "Distracted, I guess. She checked her phone a few times like she was expecting a call or a message. When I asked her about it, she just mumbled something about Jonathan and then changed the subject."

"She didn't talk about him much."

"I didn't see them together often, but I always had the impression he kind of swept her off her feet. Almost like in the fairy tales where the prince falls for the regular girl."

"Prince?" Delia sounded surprised by the description.

"Not literally. It was just that he was rich, didn't seem to do much for work, and liked to spoil Serena. He always made me think of Prince Charming."

I could think of another type of man who kept quiet about their work: criminals.

"Thanks for all your help, Tasha," I said as I helped Delia to her feet.

She looked flustered by my gratitude. "I don't feel like I was any help at all."

"I feel better knowing my cousin has such a good friend," Delia assured her.

"And now we know to work harder on getting in touch with Jonathan," I added.

"Can you ask Serena to call me when you find her? Or let me know if there's anything else I can do? Maybe talk to the police if she hasn't been in touch by tomorrow?"

There was a fine line for us to walk with Tasha now. We'd alerted her to the possible danger Serena might be in, but I didn't want her calling the cops too soon. "We'll keep in touch either way and let you know what's going on with Serena as soon as we hear anything. Maybe we'll get lucky and she managed to catch the same bug her mom has and Jonathan's taking care of her while she's too ill to speak."

"I hope it's something like that."

"Isn't it strange to wish my cousin ill like this?" Delia asked as she moved toward the door, helping to break some of the tension.

"It really is," Tasha replied with a startled laugh.

"Thanks again for all your help."

I paused to send a quick text to Brody, telling him to focus on Jonathan. Delia was already through the door when Tasha called out, "Wait!"

I turned and she was holding a business card, offering it to me with an outstretched hand. "We know how to reach you if we need anything else."

"Take it,' she insisted. "It's not mine. It's Serena's and it has her photo on it. We just had them updated a couple weeks ago, so it's a current picture. I just remembered the receptionist kept a stack of them for each of us so she could give them out at the front desk."

"Thanks," I said as I snagged it from her hand and headed for the door. I saw Delia waiting for me through the glass doors and the hairs on the back of my neck raised. The feeling that something bad was about to happen washed over me. I took in the outside surroundings. Something was setting my internal radar off and I'd learned to trust my instincts—especially since they'd saved me so many times before on missions. When I saw a black SUV with tinted windows roar in front of the building, I knew it was the cause of the alarms going off in my head.

I was already moving fast when I saw the passenger window roll down and a gloved hand holding a gun take aim right at Delia. "Get down!" I yelled, shoving the door open.

Everything happened at once. Delia turned to look at me, confusion clear on her face. The shooter fired several rounds as I ran toward her. Her body jerked, spinning around as she fell toward the ground. One arm reached out to brace for the impact and then she was down, the side of her head bouncing off the pavement as she crumpled. I wasn't sure how many times she'd been hit, but I knew I hadn't been fast enough to stop her from getting shot.

Diving over her body, I tried not to put my weight on her as I provided her with the only protection I had if the shooter fired again. I braced myself on my left arm and drew my Glock with my right, taking aim as the SUV whipped around the corner on squealing tires. By the time I'd taken aim, I didn't have a clear shot, but I could see their license plate. I committed the number to memory and lifted my body off Delia, relieved to see her looking up at me with shocked, pain-filled eyes.

CHAPTER 8

Delia

One minute, I was waiting for Blaine on the sidewalk, barely stopping myself from doing a happy dance because I'd been right about coming along, and the next, all hell broke loose. There was a series of loud popping sounds before I jerked and stumbled forward, a hot, searing pain tearing across my arm. It all happened so fast, yet it felt like time was moving in slow motion.

Thrown off balance, I was suddenly hurtling toward the ground as explosions continued to ring in my ears. My upper arm throbbed and I felt a trickle of blood dripping down my hand. I gritted my teeth in pain, fighting back shock as I tried to scramble to my feet. Then Blaine was there, his body suspended over mine as I lay there panting, tears streaming down my cheeks.

The relieved look on Blaine's face when he levered off me was unmistakable, setting butterflies off in my queasy stomach. "Where were you hit?"

"My left arm," I answered, my voice breaking halfway through my response.

His eyes darted to my arm and he did a quick scan of my body before lifting me into his arms and running toward my car.

I heard sirens, but they sounded far off. "Shouldn't we wait for an ambulance?"

His only answer was a swift shake of his head as he gently placed me in the passenger seat. He scanned the parking lot and looked back at the office before crouching down and adjusting me in the seat so he could get a look at my arm. I glanced over his head and saw Serena's co-workers peering through the glass, watching us. One of them had probably called the police when they realized what they had heard was gunfire outside their front door.

"Looks like the bullet grazed you." Blaine's tone was relieved.

"That's a good thing, right?"

"Yeah," he confirmed, pulling a knife from his front pocket and tearing a strip off the bottom of his shirt. "But we need to stop the bleeding."

He tied the fabric around my arm and the pain became even worse. "Hurts," I wheezed out.

"You need to keep pressure on it and keep your arm elevated. Slow the bleeding until I can get you to a doctor."

He didn't give me a chance to argue. He just shifted me back in the seat, strapped my seat belt on, and walked around the car, calmly and confidently. I was gaping at him while he started the engine and pulled out of the parking lot, using his turn signal and everything.

The sirens were getting louder. Help was close. "We should have waited for the police."

"Not until I know it's a safe move," he disagreed.

"Safe!" I shouted, wincing as a new jolt of pain blazed up my arm. "I think that ship has sailed and is long gone by now. To me, getting shot is the furthest thing from safe."

"There are worse things in this world than getting shot," he corrected me. "Your arm will heal, but I need you to focus on keeping pressure on the wound."

Several cop cars flew past us and I swiveled my head, watching them drive by. All my life, I'd been taught to call 9-1-1 for help. Yet, here I was, gripping the strip of cloth Blaine had tied around my arm as we drove away from the police—away from the scene of a crime. I was trusting Blaine with my life and hoping if I held on to the cloth tightly enough, some of the pain would disappear. No such luck, but at least I wasn't dripping blood anymore.

Blood.

From a bullet wound.

In my arm.

Where I'd been shot.

Holy crap.

"I was shot," I whispered, realization setting in as I trembled in my seat.

"Everything's going to be okay," Blaine tried to reassure me.

"I don't think anything will ever be okay again." I didn't see how it was possible considering the situation I found myself in.

"Don't fucking talk like that," he swore. "I should never have brought you with me in the first place, but I sure as hell will make sure you're okay."

It was clear he was blaming himself for my injury. If I were in my right mind, maybe I would be blaming him, too. Maybe I hadn't been thinking clearly since I met him. Whatever the excuse, the truth was, I didn't blame him for the bullet wound in my arm. "Don't even try to go there. You needed me with you so Serena's co-workers would open up. If I hadn't come with, Tasha might not have talked to you. And if she hadn't talked, we wouldn't have a lead right now."

"And you wouldn't have been clipped by a fucking bullet!" he roared.

Just like that, Mr. Calm and Collected left the building, replaced by Mr. Furious. I'd never seen someone so filled with rage before. I should have been terrified, but it was hard to be scared of a man who was this pissed off in my honor. Instead, it set off a flurry of butterflies in my stomach.

I held my breath until Blaine's focus shifted away from me to his phone. He called someone and explained the situation, asking for directions to somewhere he could take me to get my arm looked at. We drove through downtown and into what was most definitely a bad neighborhood with boarded up storefronts and graffiti on the buildings. I didn't understand why we were there until Blaine parked in front of a small clinic.

Everyone's eyes were on us in the waiting room, but it didn't take long before we were ushered back, even though it was already full when we arrived. As we were shown into an exam room, Blaine insisted we stay together—not that anybody was putting up much resistance to the idea. The clinic was small and didn't seem to have the same rules about privacy as a hospital would. Surprisingly, the doctor joined us a couple minutes later.

Without the help of a nurse, he removed the makeshift bandage to reveal the bullet hole in my arm. "You are aware I need to report this to the police, correct?" the doctor asked after examining the wound.

Blaine looked around the examination room before answering. "I'm aware you're *supposed* to report bullet wounds to the police, but I think *need* is too strong a word. Looks to me like there are other things you need more than the paperwork you'll have to fill out if you make that call. Things I can help you get so you'll be better equipped to provide care to your patients in the future."

The doctor's eyebrow arched in surprise as his gaze swept over us again. "What you're asking of me doesn't come cheap."

"You name your price and I'll make sure it gets paid."

My jaw dropped at Blaine's response, but the doctor took it in stride. He pulled his prescription pad out of his pocket and jotted something down before tearing it off and handing it to Blaine. After a quick glance down, Blaine nodded. "Consider it done."

"Okay," the doctor agreed before turning to me and shifting gears quickly. He was clearly more accustomed to situations like this than I was. "You're lucky. It looks like there isn't any bone or neurovascular damage, but you are going to need stitches."

"I've never had stitches before," I admitted nervously. The idea of this man sticking a needle in my throbbing arm, over and over again, freaked me out.

The doctor patted my hand gently. "I've given thousands of them in my time. I'm going to inject you with a local anesthetic before I stitch you back up so you won't feel a thing."

I felt the sting of the shot before he cleaned out my wound and stitched me up. At Blaine's insistence, he followed that up by poking, prodding, and x-raying me to ensure I hadn't done additional damage when I went down. We were both relieved to hear my wrist wasn't broken, nor were my ribs cracked. I had a small bump on the back of my head, but no signs of a concussion. The bruises were bad enough to where I was going to be sore for a while, but the doctor gave me a prescription to help with the pain, along with an antibiotic to prevent infection.

"You'll want to keep your arm elevated. Protect the wound while showering so it stays dry and change the bandage twice daily. I'd like to see you back in three days. If that's not possible, then you should see your doctor for follow-up care," he instructed, giving additional details about signs of infection and emergency care while I listened intently. "Any questions?"

I had about a million of them, but apparently Blaine thought he had it all covered. "I'll take care of her."

"That just leaves the matter of our payment arrangement," the doctor reminded Blaine.

"I can wire it to you from my phone right now."

I listened as the doctor gave him his account information and tried unsuccessfully to peek over Blaine's shoulder so I could see how much he was paying for the doctor's silence. I was worried it was a ton of money because he wouldn't let me see and then he bundled me out of there before I could ask any more questions.

After a stop at the pharmacy for my prescriptions and dressing supplies, we were finally pulling into the parking garage at the hotel. Blaine helped me up to the suite and got me settled on the couch. It was late afternoon and I was sore and tired. I wanted nothing more than to medicate myself into a deep slumber and wake up in the morning to a world where nobody thought I was dead and bad guys weren't shooting at me.

"Food, meds, and then bed," Blaine barked out.

"How about I skip the meal, take a pain pill, and crash?"

He shook the bottle of pills, rattling them. "Doc said you take these with food, so you're gonna eat something before I hand them over."

I was sitting on a couch with a bullet wound in my arm and my body half covered in bruises. My brain was spinning from everything that happened today and his words and dominating tone should have pissed me off instead of turning me on. Heck, even if he stripped down naked I shouldn't feel anything other than pain right now, but my body apparently wasn't willing to listen to reason. Neither was my brain. Not when it came to Blaine.

"I guess I'm going to let you cook for me after all."

A smile spread across his face, giving him an unexpectedly playful look, making him even more attractive. I felt like it was my reward for being able to focus long enough to recall exactly what I'd said during our argument earlier. "Then I guess I better do my best to make sure it doesn't taste crappy."

"Can you manage sandwiches? Or something else quick? I don't think I'm going to be able to last much longer without that pain pill you're holding hostage."

"Absolutely, baby." I shivered at his use of the endearment. I'd liked it when he'd called me baby when we were at the real estate office, but I thought it was just part of our act. Hearing him say it again here, in the suite, when we were all alone, was even better. It was just for him and me—not because he was putting on a show for someone else. It made the word more meaningful, as though something had shifted between us when I was shot.

"I'm going to change while you're making lunch." My clothes were destroyed. I wanted the bloody mess off my body and thrown in the trash. Unfortunately, it was a heck of a lot easier in theory. I was starting to feel the pain and it took me longer than I thought it would to get out of my clothes, leaving me standing in just my panties when Blaine knocked on the door.

"Lunch is ready. You need any help in there?"

I grabbed the comforter off the bed and wrapped it around myself before answering the door. "Do you have a button-down shirt I can borrow?"

Blaine's eyes flared with heat as they scanned down my legs, traveling back up again and pausing at my chest like maybe he had x-ray vision and could see through the blanket. "Only the one I was wearing when I hopped on the plane, but you're welcome to borrow it."

When he bent over to dig through his bag, my eyes were drawn to his ass, lovingly hugged by his jeans. My reaction time was slow and he caught me staring when he turned around with a white dress shirt in his hands. His smug grin was enough for me to know he had a good idea of exactly what I'd been looking at.

"Thanks," I whispered, looking down at the floor as I felt heat sweep across my cheeks.

"Get settled in bed and I'll bring in the sandwiches."

Taking the shirt from him, I waited until he walked out of the room to drop the comforter back on the bed. When I'd asked to borrow a shirt from him, I wasn't expecting a tuxedo shirt—especially not one that smelled like him. It perfectly suited my purposes though: big enough so it hung mid-thigh and I was able to roll up the sleeve past the bandage on my arm. With the buttons, I didn't have to worry about pulling it over my head later if the pain worsened. The best part was it made me feel like I had him wrapped around me.

I was pulling the covers around me when he came back into the room, carrying a plate stacked high with sandwiches in one hand and a tall glass of milk, of all things, in the other. "Milk?"

"It will speed the entry of the pain pills into your digestive system and minimize stomach upset."

My nose scrunched up. Milk was one of my least favorite drinks. "You seem pretty knowledgeable about medical stuff."

"Being a SEAL, you learn a bit about medicine. Putting pressure on a wound, stitching a cut, sinking an IV. You have to be prepared for all kinds of things in the field."

"They teach you big, bad tough guys to drink milk in the SEALs?" I asked as I took a sandwich from the plate.

"Nah," he answered, shaking his head. "My mom taught me that trick when I was a kid."

Blaine's voice held such warmth when he mentioned his mom. It showed a softer side to him—one I found appealing. "Were you sick often when you were little?"

"I was as healthy as a horse when I wasn't breaking one bone or another."

It was difficult to picture him as a young boy. His personality was larger than life. He was too commanding to think of him as someone's beloved son, but I felt like I could listen to him talk about his childhood for hours. I kept asking questions as we ate our sandwiches in bed. When mine was half gone, Blaine handed me two pills. By the time I finished, I was fighting to keep my eyes open and my words started to slur as I tried to learn as much as I could about Blaine while he was willing to answer my questions. Eventually, he stretched out on the bed, his back against the headboard, and pulled me against his chest. Between the warmth of his body, the soothing sound of his voice, and the pain pills, it was impossible to resist the pull of sleep. I drifted off. And then the dreams came.

I wasn't sure how long I'd slept, but the room was dark when my body jerked as I awoke with the sound of gunshots ringing in my ears. My heart was racing as

I frantically searched the room until I realized it was just a bad dream. The moment Blaine's arms closed around me, I felt protected and safe—like he was standing guard between me and the world. No other man had ever safeguarded me in quite the same way, except maybe my dad. The extremeness of our situation might have been partially responsible for my feelings, but I didn't care. I was invested enough to want to see what happened next. Then I gazed into Blaine's eyes and saw the tortured look as he stared at the bandage on my arm and I knew—even though this thing growing between us was still undefined and incredibly new, his feelings were as deeply engaged as mine.

CHAPTER 9

Blaine

"I'm okay," she whispered, chanting it over and over again.

Her voice shook and I could see the panic she was trying to hide from me. She'd been so peaceful when she fell asleep in my arms a few hours ago. Cuddling had never been my thing, but I found myself laying there with her until I eventually fell asleep, too. When she started to twitch, I woke up and tried to soothe her, knowing she needed as much rest as she could get to help speed the healing process along. I knew I should step away and give her some time to regroup, but I couldn't force my body to move. Wanting to put her at ease, I kept my breathing slow and willed my body to relax. After a few minutes, her breathing slowed to match mine.

I took a deep breath, drawing her scent into my lungs as I ran my palms over her back. She'd been shot. A bullet had ripped through her silky soft skin and it had happened under my watch. I didn't know if I would ever forgive myself, or if she would ever forgive me for putting her at risk.

"It's almost time for another pain pill," I murmured into her hair.

"Not yet."

"Now, baby," I insisted. "I don't want you in pain."

"I'll take one in a minute, but they muddle my brain and I want you to know this is me talking and not the medication," she mumbled into my shirt before tilting her head back and looking me straight in the eyes. "Please don't blame yourself for this."

"Who the fuck else should I blame?" I growled.

"The person who shot me," she replied, like it was the obvious answer.

"It's not that simple, Delia," I sighed. "I'm the one who gave Serena the contact who helped her check into the hotel under your name in the first place. The one who talked you into not calling the police. I drove down to that real estate office because it would make it easier for me to get the answers I needed and then I let you walk outside without me—without any protection."

"It doesn't seem that simple to me," she argued. "Serena's the one who made the decision to use my name, not you. She pulled me into this, not you. Everything else after that is on me. Ultimately, I make my own decisions. So, if you aren't willing to blame the bad guys for this mess, then I guess you're going to have to share the responsibility with me."

She was hopped up on pain meds, her face was pale, her eyes were bruised, and she had a bullet wound in her arm, yet I didn't think I had ever seen a woman look more beautiful in my life as she argued with me. Suddenly, the danger I'd unwittingly dragged her into didn't matter. The fact that we'd only known each other for a day didn't make a difference either. I wasn't able to keep my distance any longer, not after watching her hit the pavement after taking a bullet. Not after that brief moment when I wasn't sure where she'd been hit—whether she'd live or die. All that mattered right now was my need to touch her. I had to show her I cared. Show her I wanted her.

Reaching up to cup her cheek with one hand, I swept my thumb gently over the bruise forming on her cheek. She drew in a deep breath at the touch of my fingers. Her gaze flicked down to my mouth before moving back to my eyes. Her pulse fluttered faster in her throat. As I recognized the heat in her gaze, I felt an intense wave of possessive desire shoot through me.

Sliding my palm to the back of her head, I was driven by my need to protect this woman. To make her mine in the most primal way. Leaning down, I covered her mouth with mine. I captured her soft gasp, sliding my tongue along the seam of her lips and driving it inside when her lips parted beneath mine. When she made a soft sound in the back of her throat and pressed her curvy body against me, my hardened cock twitched, pressing against my zipper.

I was aching for her. Nothing would make me happier than to peel away her clothes and taste every inch of her. I wanted to make her beg for my cock. She moaned and I realized it wasn't in pleasure but pain. With a groan, I pulled back and searched her eyes. Although they were heated with desire and glazed over from our kiss, I knew she was in pain. As deeply as I regretted it, now wasn't the time to move this any further.

I moved away, but her whimper of protest was almost enough to make me change my mind.

"Don't you want me?" she whispered.

"You have no idea how much I want you," I assured her. "Unfortunately, now's not the right time for this."

"But..." I pressed my finger to her lips and then the ringing of my phone saved me.

"I need to take this call. It's probably Brody letting me know when his flight lands," I explained, reaching over to grab the bottle of pain medication from the nightstand. "It's time for another pill. I'll get you some water and a snack."

I swiftly pressed my lips against hers one last time before leaving the bed and answering the phone. "You on your way?"

"Already landed." His answer should have surprised me, but it didn't. He was probably out the door and headed to the airport fifteen minutes after I asked him to come. "I'll be at the hotel in about fifteen minutes unless you need me to pick something up on my way."

"I think we've got everything we need."

"Then I guess the cozy twosome will be a threesome sooner rather than later."

Brody's sense of humor was quirky and it never failed to amuse me even in the direst of situations. But I didn't find his use of the word "threesome" in reference to Delia the slightest bit funny. He didn't give me a chance to bust his ass over it before he hung up, though. The bastard.

"You forgot my water and snack," Delia said. I turned to find her standing behind me in the doorway, still dressed in my shirt, her arm cradled protectively against her chest. "I could really use it. My arm's starting to throb again."

I grabbed a bottle from the fridge, twisted the cap off the top, and brought it over to her. "Here you go." Then I dug in the fridge for some cheese and grabbed crackers out of the pantry.

"Thanks." She smiled at me before popping a pill into her mouth and chasing it with a gulp of the water.

My eyes lingered on her legs for a moment, appreciating the view—one I didn't plan to share with my best friend. "You need to pull on some pants. Brody will be here soon."

"That was fast." She tilted her head, looking confused. "At least, I think it was. How long was I asleep?"

"It's only been a few hours."

"Doesn't Brody live in Vegas like you?" she asked as she snagged a piece of cheese.

"Yeah," I confirmed. "But I sent him a text asking him to come before we left the clinic and he has access to a private jet."

"Then I guess I better get some pants on, but I'm taking this with me," she said as she swept up the cheese and crackers before walking out of the kitchen.

It was a good thing she hadn't argued because by the time she came back out of the bedroom, Brody was knocking on the door.

"The cavalry has arrived!" His greeting was said with a laugh, but his eyes didn't hold any humor—not until he caught sight of Delia. "Aren't you going to introduce us, Saint?"

"Saint?" Delia repeated.

"Blaine didn't share his nickname with you, darling?" Brody looked between us, his eyebrow raised and a smirk on his face.

"He didn't." Delia flashed a little smile at my best friend, making the dimple in her right cheek appear. Her eyes didn't linger on the visible scars on his face and I was proud of her for not reacting the same way I'd seen other women do, by flinching. Brody's eyes did a quick scan of Delia, lingering briefly on her chest, his expression clearly showing appreciation for her body. A twinge of jealousy flared to life inside me, something I wasn't accustomed to feeling for any woman—let alone over the man I trusted more than anyone else in this world. "But I'm sure there's an interesting story behind it."

"That there is," Brody confirmed. "Maybe I'll even share it with you one day."

"Not today?" Delia asked.

"Unfortunately, I've got other news to share today." Just like that, my playful best friend switched back to the serious operator I'd seen on all our missions, meaning he didn't have anything good to tell me. "And I think you'll want to be sitting down for this, brother."

"Shit," I muttered as we moved toward the living room. Delia and I sat together on the couch and she reached out to grab my hand. "Was it the boyfriend?"

"Considering his dead body turned up this morning, I'd say it's a damn good possibility he was involved somehow," Brody answered.

"Fuck," I hissed. "A dead body can't answer questions and I could really use some right about now."

"You're not going to like one of the answers I have for you," Brody warned.

"Serena?"

He nodded. "Still nothing on her credit cards or cell phone and the body in the morgue fits her description perfectly. I spent the flight going over the security tapes I pulled from the hotel's system and ran her photo through facial recognition. It was a match to the woman who checked in under Delia's name."

"No sign of her leaving?" I couldn't stop myself from asking even though I already knew the answer. He would never have told me this if there was even a remote chance she'd left that hotel in anything other than a body bag.

"I'm sorry, man."

Delia's hand tightened around mine, offering comfort. "There's no chance at all?" she asked in a soft voice.

"No." Memories of Serena played through my mind: our shared childhood, the time we spent together as a couple, the meal we shared when I saw her before I left for my first mission.

Delia's hand squeezed again before she let go. "I'm feeling tired again from the pain pill. I think I'm going to lay down for a little bit, give you guys some time."

My eyes followed her as she walked to the bedroom, her gaze locking with mine when she turned. Time seemed to stand still until she stepped to the side and closed the door.

"I wish I had better news." Brody's voice brought me out of my head and back to reality.

"And your man? The one who helped her?"

"Still haven't been able to reach him. It's possible they connected her to him and he's on the run or they took him out, too." He shrugged his shoulders. "I'll keep working that angle, but even if we find him, he won't be able to give us much other than confirming what I've already discovered about Serena using Delia's identity. He's just a papers guy. He wouldn't have wanted to get involved beyond that. Too much trouble and outside his area of expertise."

"Then how the fuck are we supposed to figure out who the hell *they* are?"

"I'll work on gaining access to the boyfriend's computer remotely so I can see what he was into. Maybe I'll find a lead on him."

We spent the next hour combing through the background report on Jonathan again, looking for anything that might point us in the right direction. "We need to follow the money trail. Something isn't right about it."

"I think you're right," Brody agreed. "I'll add that to my list of things to do tonight while you check on your girl."

"My girl?"

"Don't pretend you don't know exactly what I'm talking about. Unless you aren't going to do anything about that?" Brody asked, nodding toward the bedroom.

"You just confirmed Serena's dead, her boyfriend was murdered, Delia was shot this morning, and we still don't have any idea what the hell is going on. Now isn't the time for me to start something with Delia."

"I wouldn't wait too long if I were you," Brody warned. "A woman like that? Some man is bound to come along and sweep her off her feet if you don't pull your head out of your ass and do it first."

Mine. I was startled by the thought as it rolled through my head. I'd been attracted to her since the first moment I'd laid eyes on her, even though I was swamped by grief at the knowledge that finding Delia alive meant Serena was most likely dead. Maybe if I'd been thinking more clearly, I would have sent Delia away for her own safety. One phone call to Damian was all it would have taken, but the idea of sending her to my boss made me feel a possessiveness I'd never felt before. Working for him over the past year meant I had plenty of opportunities to see how women responded to him. There wasn't a chance in hell I ever wanted to see desire in Delia's eyes when she looked at him. I wanted it for myself, even though I felt like an asshole for feeling like this.

"Any asshole who thinks he's going to take her away from me is bound to get his head ripped off," I growled.

"Then what the fuck are you doing out here with me when you could be in there with her? We both know I've got this covered. You're just going to hold me back if you try to help me. You're slow as shit and talkative as hell when you're behind a keyboard. Didn't we already learn this lesson?"

"I guess we did," I agreed reluctantly, thinking about the mission where we almost didn't evade capture because I distracted Brody while he was trying to do his hacker thing.

"Let me put it this way, Saint. There's three of us, one king bed big enough for two in that bedroom, and a couch out here that will only fit one. Someone's gotta join her in there. You want it to be me or you?"

"It damn well won't be you," I hissed as I jumped to my feet and stormed toward the bedroom. "Stay away from Delia."

The moment I saw her on the bed, my anger at Brody faded. I knew he was playing me—pushing me toward her because he thought it was best for me. And when she opened her arms to me, I gave up trying to resist this thing between us. The logical side of me knew this wasn't the time for seduction, but I was past the point of caring. We were safe for now, but you never knew what was coming around the corner. I wasn't going to wait any longer.

No time like the present, I thought as I strode toward the bed and climbed in beside her. My shirt was riding up her thighs and I tugged the sheet lower so I could trace my finger over her panties. When she moaned and let her head fall back onto the pillow, I took that as permission to keep going.

"You're so fucking sexy. I need a taste. Just let me taste you." Pulling her panties down her legs, I followed their path and nibbled her creamy skin along the way. Once they were out of my way, I parted her thighs and slowly sank a finger into her pussy. As I stroked inside, she soaked my hand with her desire. Unable to resist any longer, I leaned forward to suck lightly on her clit and hummed in pleasure when her hips bucked underneath me.

"Ouch," she hissed.

I tore my mouth away from her pussy and found her cradling her arm. "What happened, baby?"

"I forgot."

I hated knowing she was in pain, but I felt like thumping my chest in triumph at the knowledge that I'd given her so much pleasure she'd somehow forgotten she was shot earlier today. "On your knees."

Her lips curved slightly at my command. "My knees?"

"You heard me," I rasped, rolling onto my back and patting my chest. "You'll be more comfortable up here while I lick and suck and tease you until you're coming on my tongue."

"Up there?" she questioned, and I took great satisfaction in the fact that her voice wasn't steady. "What exactly do you have in mind?"

"I want you on your knees, straddling my face." My voice held a bark of command as I started getting impatient for another taste of her. I licked my lips, savoring her flavor—anticipating what it would feel like when she was hovering over me and I was able to hold her ass in my hands, pulling her pussy down to my mouth. "And I want it now."

My cock was already straining against my boxers, but when she raised to her knees, it twitched and I felt a drop of pre-come seep from the tip. "What about what I want?" she asked.

"Trust me, baby. I'm about to give you exactly what you want."

"And if I want more?" she asked huskily, her eyes raking down my body and lingering on my hard-on.

"Delia," I groaned. She was hell on my principles. I was already going further than I should while she was taking pain pills. "If you still want me to fuck you tomorrow, I'll be more than happy to give us both what we want. But not tonight. Not when you don't know what you're asking for."

She cocked her head at me like she was trying to figure me out before a small, secret smile tilted her lips. "Fine, my bossy sailor. No sex for me tonight, but you're not the only one who gets to lick, suck, and tease."

Before my brain caught up with the meaning of her words, she had moved so her knees were planted on either side of my head. Her thighs were open and her pussy was mere inches from my lips. But she was facing opposite of what I'd intended. Leaning down, she braced herself on her good arm and ran her cheek along the length of my cock. My plan to give without taking flew out the window when I felt her hot breath on my hardened length.

"Any sign of pain from you and I'll have to flip you onto your back and tie your arm down so you don't hurt yourself," I growled.

"Is that supposed to be a threat?" she murmured, her eyes heated as she looked at me through the space between our bodies. "Because it doesn't scare me. Quite the opposite, in fact. It kind of makes me want to cry out just so you have an excuse to tie me up."

Outside of bed, Delia was one of the nicest women I'd ever met. Sexy as hell, but so damn sweet. I would never have guessed her gentle exterior hid an adventurous seductress. "Maybe another time."

"Promises, promises." She lowered her hips slightly and shivered above me as I traced my finger along the seam of her inner thigh.

Turning my head, I kissed her soft skin and tightened my hold on her thighs as she jerked in surprise. "Easy, baby. I don't want you to hurt yourself. Lay your arm over my leg."

When I felt the weight of her arm on my thigh, I slowly widened my legs, shifting until her arm was outstretched and away from my hips. I didn't want to jostle her if my hips jerked.

"There you go, baby. You can play all you want as long as it doesn't bother your arm." I lightly trailed my tongue along her pussy lips, deliberately letting my breath fan over her damp flesh.

"Blaine," she moaned.

I teased her until she widened her legs further and groaned when my lips made it to her clit, nipping at it. "I'm gonna make you come so hard, your juices are going to run down my face."

Her only response was a jerk of her hips before she pushed my boxers down my hips, freeing my cock, and then laying her arm over my thigh again. Her movements were clumsy since she was bracing all of her weight on her good arm. "Are you sure your arm is okay for this?"

Her fingers wrapped around me, cutting off my line of thought. Then her warm breath teased the tip of my cock, her tongue flicking out to taste the drop of pre-come there. I clenched my jaw in an effort to gain control over the urge to drive myself past her lips and deep into her throat. It was easy to picture how her lips would look locked around my cock as I thrust between them. My balls tightened and I needed to focus on getting her off before I blew my load and embarrassed myself.

Knowing the best defense was a good offense, I tightened my hands around her hips and held her in place while I parted her with my tongue. I swatted an ass cheek before sliding my hand lower and circling her opening with a finger. Her back arched as she cried out, gasping my name.

I hadn't counted on her determination to give while she received. She sucked my cock deep, her fingernails digging into my thigh as she slid her mouth up and down my hardened length. My thighs tightened, my breath caught in my lungs, and my body shuddered in response to her ministrations.

"Fuck, Delia," I hissed out in warning.

I eased a finger into her wet heat, eliciting a moan that vibrated against my cock. Timing my motions, I thrust my finger in and out of her in sync with the slide of her mouth on my shaft. I gave her clit one last lick before sucking it into my mouth, adding a second finger on the next thrust. Her hips jerked back and forth as she rode my tongue while her mouth kept working me. When I thrust upwards, she moaned hungrily against my cock. The sound snapped what little control I had left.

I searched out the soft, spongy spot inside her and rubbed it relentlessly. There was no way I was going over the edge without dragging her with me. My vision greyed and my body shuddered as my balls drew up against my body. Her scream of release echoed through the room as my orgasm tore through me. My head slammed down against the mattress, my hips thrusting into her mouth as I rode out the waves.

Nothing had prepared me for the satisfaction I felt when she swallowed my come, licking her lips as she changed position and cuddled against my chest.

CHAPTER 10

Delia

I couldn't stop grinning like a fool as I traced my finger lightly over Blaine's chest. I'd more than likely pay for our activity later when the pain pill wore off, but the orgasm he'd given me was definitely worth the discomfort. It had been too long since I had climaxed with the help of someone other than my vibrator. I'd probably pushed myself too hard with the decision to give Blaine the blowjob, but I couldn't help myself. The second I saw the outline of his dick straining against his boxers when I got up on my knees, I wanted a taste of him for myself. And I wasn't willing to wait.

Sleeping with a guy this soon after meeting him wasn't normal for me. Then again, my life hadn't been the same old, same old from the moment I walked into my home and found Blaine there. I really wanted to blame everything that had happened for the recklessness of my decision to hop into bed with him, but I knew it was more than that. I just hoped Blaine didn't get the wrong idea about me.

"I'm not a slut," I muttered.

"Come again?"

Blaine's voice was huskier than usual and so damn sexy I almost forgot what I'd said. It was too easy to fall into a daze around him. "Nothing," I mumbled.

His hand gripped my chin and tilted my head up until I met his gaze. "You think I couldn't tell it had been a while for you? With how snug your pussy was around my finger and how hard you came for me?"

"Blaine!" I gasped.

"All I'm saying is you're not just an easy lay to me."

He probably meant it as reassurance, but his delivery could use a heck of a lot of work. "Just?" I repeated. "Let me get this straight, see if I understand. You're saying I'm an easy lay but I'm also more?"

"It figures, you being an author, you'd focus on the one word in the sentence that could piss you off."

"Well, then, maybe you shouldn't have worded it that way." I levered off his chest and tried to get off the bed before he pulled me back onto the bed by his side, not gently, but carefully enough to make sure I landed on my good side.

"Fuck, baby. You're hot when you're angry with me. You just made me come hard and you're still able to get my cock hard just by throwing attitude my way. I'm starting to think it's a good thing you like to argue."

"Why in the world would that be good?" I'd never been one to argue. I wasn't comfortable with confrontation. I was more the 'suffer in silence' type—except, apparently, with Blaine. This was yet another new thing for me since meeting him.

"We just proved the chemistry between us is off the charts." He looked at me like he was waiting for me to agree. I certainly couldn't argue against his point so I nodded my head. "And I'm willing to bet the make-up sex will be un-fucking-believable."

Damn if that didn't make me wet again.

"Blaine." His name was a breathy sigh, the anger draining from me as suddenly as it came.

"I'm not used to sugar-coating my words, Delia. I call 'em like I see 'em and sometimes I can be a dick."

This wasn't news to me, not after the way he'd ended our conversation this morning. "Is that supposed to be an apology?"

His chest shook as he laughed, the sound wrapping around me as I felt the reverberations on my cheek. "More like a heads up. You wanna do this thing with me, you better be prepared to brace and take me as I am—in bed and out."

"This thing?"

"Baby, you just gave yourself to me. When you got on your knees and crawled over my body so I could eat your pussy while you sucked my dick? That was the start of something between us. I'm not sure what to call it. Words are your thing, not mine. Feel free to put a name to it."

A loud knock on the door interrupted us, a startling reminder that Brody was in the other room. "I hate to interrupt your fun, but I think I found something."

"Do you think he could hear us?" I whispered, horrified, thinking about how loudly I had screamed when I came.

"Yup," Brody answered through the door.

I rolled away from Blaine and pulled the sheet over my face, groaning in embarrassment.

"We'll be out in a second," Blaine called to Brody before rubbing my back. "I should have warned you, his hearing is crazy good. It saved our asses a time or two, but it sure as hell can make things awkward in close quarters."

"Please tell me he's not staying here. He has another suite, right? One which doesn't share a wall with this room?" I panicked, my words bursting from me in a rush.

"He's not just here to help gather intel. He could do that just as easily from Vegas. I asked him to come because you were shot and I need someone I trust to have our backs. Which means he stays close and rides the couch 'til this is over."

"No more orgasms for me," I sighed, disappointment coloring my tone. As wrong as it might have been, considering the situation, I'd been looking forward to spending more time between the sheets with Blaine— and soon. My climax had been good, but I knew it would be better with him deep inside me.

"You want me to take the time now to prove how wrong you are about that?" The promise in his gravelly voice had my pussy convulsing.

"No," I answered, even though it was the exact opposite of what I really wanted.

"You sure? Because I'm up for the challenge." He gripped my hand and slid it down his body, wrapping my fist around his hardened length.

"You don't have screaming orgasms with your friends listening right outside the door." My protest was a half-hearted contradiction to the motion of my hand as it glided up his shaft.

He moved until his face was within an inch of mine, trapping my hand around him with his own and squeezing gently. "Wrong, baby. I'm not going to wait until he's gone to feel your pussy wrapped around my dick. When I'm inside you, you will scream my name, and I don't give a fuck who hears us. Neither will you."

"Arrogant bastard."

"It isn't arrogance if it's true." He dropped a quick kiss on my lips before climbing out of bed and pulling his jeans on. "I'll prove it to you later. Right now, we better go see what Brody found before he decides to come in here and I have to kick his ass for seeing you naked."

"I wouldn't want to be the reason you beat up your best friend."

Blaine picked up the shirt I'd been wearing and tossed it at me. "Wouldn't be the first time one of us punched the other and I'm sure it wouldn't be the last."

He grabbed a t-shirt from his bag and pulled it over his head, waiting until I was dressed before opening the door. "I'll be out in a second. I need to brush my teeth."

His gaze dropped to my mouth and heat flared in his eyes. I had no doubt he knew exactly why I wanted to brush my teeth. The wicked gleam in his eye and smug tilt of his lips warned me he was about to say something bound to piss me off again. "Out!" I ordered, pointing at the door. "As much fun as it seems to be for you, I don't have the energy to get into another argument right now."

"Maybe later," he murmured before the door shut behind him.

"That man is going to drive me insane," I muttered to myself. "But holy crap it would totally be worth it."

****

By the time I made it into the living room, the guys were standing at the kitchen counter staring at Brody's laptop. I took a moment to appreciate the sight of the two of them together, their broad shoulders almost touching as they leaned against the granite countertop. My eyes were drawn to Blaine, but that didn't mean I couldn't appreciate the eye candy that was Brody Slater. He was a couple inches shorter than Blaine, but filled out a pair of jeans just as well.

"If you're done ogling, you might as well come over here and join us." Brody's voice was filled with humor, but my eyes jerked up to catch Blaine glaring at me. I'd obviously been caught checking out Brody's ass.

The moment I made it over to them, Blaine tossed his arm over my shoulder, pulling me close. It was a territorial move, one that clearly staked a claim.

"Why don't you just pee on her leg and get it over with?"

"Fuck you," Blaine muttered without any heat. Looking up at him, I was surprised to find his cheeks tinted red with embarrassment—he didn't seem like the kind of guy who was fazed by much.

When he didn't loosen his hold, I settled into his embrace and nodded my head toward the laptop. "What did I miss?"

"I found some suspicious activity online. Looks like the boyfriend was dirty," Brody said.

"What kind of activity?"

"Regular visits to a bitcoin exchange, some activity on the deep web. Places your average person wouldn't know about let alone visit online," Blaine replied.

"And it might explain why I haven't been able to trace the source of his income yet."

I felt like they were speaking in a different language. "Deep web?"

"There's a part of the internet where people can remain anonymous. It's called the deep web," Brody explained.

"And bitcoins? That sounds techy too."

"Bitcoins act like a currency or commodity. You can have bitcoins just like you can have gold or cash. The difference is bitcoins exist electronically rather than physically. So, if you have bitcoins and you want dollars, you have to find someone who has dollars and wants bitcoins to make a trade. That's where the exchanges come into play."

Brody's explanation was clear and concise, easy enough for even me to understand. "Sounds like you've had to give that explanation before."

"He's used to translating his tech talk into English for me."

Brody looked at Blaine and shook his head. "You understand more than most of the other guys, don't play dumb now."

"What about Serena?" I asked.

"Everything I've found so far indicates she was clean."

"Brody's being generous," Blaine growled. "I'd like to think she didn't know what her boyfriend was into, but we don't know that. I really hope she didn't know he was dirty. She sure didn't seem to mind him spending his money on her and I would hate to think she'd changed so much that she didn't care where the money came from."

Blaine's voice was filled with pain. I turned in his arms and hugged him tightly, wanting to offer comfort and take away some of his hurt. "She knew how honorable you are, right?"

"Yeah."

"Then it stands to reason she wouldn't have pulled you into this if she was one of the bad guys. Why ask for help from a hero when you're wearing a black hat? It doesn't make sense."

"Even though she was the kind of woman who wanted the sweet life, it doesn't mean she went dark to get it, brother," Brody added.

"I hope you two are right," Blaine sighed.

"How about we assume the best but prepare for the worst when it comes to Serena's involvement in this?" I suggested.

Blaine's arms tightened around me. "SEALs are always prepared for the worst."

"What else can we do to prepare? How about we try to talk through everything we know?"

"Blaine and I have worked the problem over and over again. I don't see how walking through it again with you is going to help," Brody grumbled.

"I may not have been a SEAL, but I'm a woman. I have an advantage when it comes to thinking like Serena," I pointed out.

"Definitely a woman," Blaine murmured, the heat in his eyes letting me know he was thinking about our time in bed together.

"And I'm an author," I pushed forward, resisting the urge to drag him back to bed to prove exactly how much of a woman I was. "So I'm pretty good with plotting things out. Maybe if we tackle this like a book we'll be able to come up with something you guys can follow up on."

"It's worth a shot," Blaine conceded.

"You're lead on this one. If you want to go through it again with Delia, then I guess that's what we're going to do." Although Brody seemed easygoing at first, I was beginning to think there was more than what met the eye with him.

"So, what are the facts as we know them?"

"Serena knew she was in trouble. She had time to get away from whoever was after her. She reached out to Blaine for help via text. He couldn't make it to her fast enough so he sent her to a guy I found online who presumably got her a credit card and identification in Delia's name so she could check into the hotel. At some point between when she left her home and the morning Blaine arrived, someone broke in and tore the place apart. They managed to locate her at the hotel, beat the shit out of her, and shot her multiple times before the kill shot to the head," Brody said, beginning the rundown of information.

"What about the timing of her boyfriend's death?" Blaine asked.

Brody pulled something up on his computer before he answered. "The initial estimate by the medical examiner places his death around the time you got the first text from Serena."

"Maybe she witnessed his murder and somehow got away?" I asked.

"No, that doesn't fit the details of their deaths. Her boyfriend was a clean shot to the head, execution style. No signs of torture, but there was a call from his cell phone to her office line a couple hours before she texted me." Blaine filled in some more gaps.

"I did a little more digging into his cell phone records. That call was made from Macon, where his body was found," Brody added.

"So, it could have been a warning from her boyfriend that made her run?" This rundown was a good idea. It allowed me to listen to the facts at hand with a certain degree of detachment and play them through my head like the plot of a book. "They were looking for something at her apartment. What about his place?"

"Blaine didn't search his home, but the cop on the boyfriend's murder didn't mention anything in his notes about a break in," Brody answered.

"Do I want to know how you have access to a cop's notes?" I asked.

"You don't."

"Plausible deniability," Blaine added.

"Okie dokie. If the bad guys searched her place but not his and tortured her but not him, what does that tell us?"

Brody's approving look and Blaine's quick squeeze made me thankful I'd forged ahead and ignored the fact that the source of their information was illegal.

"She had something they wanted," Blaine answered. "How the fuck didn't I think of that already?"

"And, if I had to guess, they haven't found it yet," Brody added.

"Or they wouldn't have been outside her office."

Realization finally struck. "Where they saw me, thought I was Serena, and shot me?"

"Yes, it's the most likely scenario," Blaine confirmed.

I shook my head, trying to focus on the topic at hand instead of dwelling on the fact I'd gotten shot because the bad guys thought I was someone else. "Whatever they were looking for, it couldn't have been in her house or the hotel room. She might have told them where it was during the beating, but that doesn't make sense. Why would they have been at her office?"

"Unless she hid it there and they went to retrieve it," Brody suggested.

"No, that doesn't fit," Blaine disagreed. "If she'd told them where to find whatever she was hiding, they would have been certain it was her they'd killed in the hotel room. They wouldn't have had any reason to shoot at Delia."

"Where the hell did she hide it then?"

An idea popped into my head, but it was so crazy, it didn't seem like it could even be possible. "She liked my books. Thought of my name when she needed a way to hide herself away from the bad guys. What if she used something from one of my books to hide whatever they wanted from them?"

Blaine turned me in his arms and looked down at me, confusion clear on his face. "What do you mean?"

"We don't know what she was hiding from them, but if it was small enough, she might have thought about a scene from one of my books. The hero knows the bad guys are closing in on him so he mails himself the evidence he needs to take them down in case he can't get away from them."

"That would never work in real life," Brody scoffs. "Too many things could go wrong."

"Did it work in your book?" Blaine asked.

I nodded in response, too irritated to answer because Brody's disbelief stung my pride. Blaine's head lifted and he looked at Brody. "Serena wasn't a trained operative. She would have made decisions like a civilian and for one reason or another, Delia seems to have been in her comfort zone. Just like I was."

Something passed between the two men before Brody sighed deeply. "Shit. It's going to be like looking for a needle in a fucking haystack if it hasn't been delivered yet. And we'll have to avoid the police. The Macon cops are bound to be looking for Serena by now since she was their victim's girlfriend and the last call he made was to her."

"Maybe not," I interrupted. "The hero in my book—he didn't mail the package to his home or work. He knew the bad guys would search those places if they managed to kill him."

"Where did he mail it to then?" Blaine asked.

"A hotel where he'd stayed several times and the front desk staff knew him. He'd been there often enough he knew they'd hold onto it until his next stay."

The disbelief on the guys' faces would have been comical had we not been discussing murder and mayhem.

"Are you thinking what I'm thinking?" Brody asked Blaine.

"Yeah, if she sent something to the Hilton, we're going to have a hell of a time getting our hands on it."

It was a problem we spent the rest of the day and night working on, finally coming up with a solution Blaine wasn't thrilled about but eventually agreed was the best plan—one that involved me staying behind. The risk of someone at the hotel recognizing me was too high.

CHAPTER 11

Blaine

The last time I entered this hotel, I'd expected to meet Serena, talk to her about some problem she was probably exaggerating, and help her solve it in no time flat. Now, Brody and I were walking in, fake badges clipped to our belts, in the hope our wild guess was right and we'd somehow be able to locate a clue she may or may not have left behind before she died.

"We're really gonna do it this way?"

"Yes, I'm sure," he sighed. "Chill out, brother. There's a difference between winging it and going in with a plan to see what happens. Nobody in there has any reason to question the story we're going to spin for them. We go in, see if the front desk is holding a package under Delia's name, collect it as evidence for an ongoing investigation, and then we get out."

"Our plan sounds an awful lot like winging it to me."

After he hadn't been able to find any mention of a package in the police reports, Brody had hacked into the hotel's system to see if he could find a record of one. When he came up empty, he hatched this plan and floated it to me. It sounded like crap to me, but when Delia woke up and heard the plan, she sided with Brody. She was persuasive in her argument, and the two of them managed to sway me to their way of

133

thinking. The next thing I knew, Brody had procured badges and a couple suits were delivered to the suite. Then Delia handed her keys over to me so Brody and I could head over to the hotel.

There wasn't much traffic, which wasn't a surprise since the sun hadn't risen yet. I was the one who had insisted we hit the hotel early, when the front desk would be staffed with the fewest employees. I didn't expect there to be many guests downstairs this time of day, so it was our best bet to get in and out cleanly.

As we got out of the car, Brody flashed his badge at the valet. "Leave the car where it is. We won't be here long." His voice held authority and the valet accepted the order for what it was. "Here's to hoping the front desk staff is as easy to con as that guy."

"Sometimes it's better to be lucky than good."

"You know I prefer to be both," Brody retorted as we reached the front desk.

"Good morning, gentlemen. Welcome to the Hilton. How can I help you today?" The girl was young, pretty, and her eyes were locked on Brody like she was picturing him naked. He flashed me a smirk before turning his attention to the girl.

"Morning, beautiful. My partner and I were hoping you could help us out," he drawled.

"Partner?" she repeated, her gaze darting to me before returning to Brody.

"Not like that, darlin'," he scoffed, flashing her the badge he'd acquired. "Atlanta PD, homicide division."

"Oh." Her sigh was relieved. "I'm not sure how I can help if this is about that author. This is my first day back from vacation."

"Vacation? Don't break my heart and tell me you went away with a boyfriend."

Brody's tone was as flirtatious as his words, and the girl was quick to blush and tuck a lock of hair behind her ear. If there was a package back there with Delia's name on it, I had no doubt she'd happily hand it over to Brody. I stood back, kept quiet, and let him work his magic.

"I don't have a boyfriend," she answered, her voice breathless.

"I find that hard to believe, you being so pretty," he said before looking over at me. "It's too bad I'm here on official police business. Maybe I'll have to come back again for personal reasons."

"I'm working the next five days straight," she offered.

"I'll keep that in mind, sugar," he purred. "And I have to admit, I'm no longer irritated our anonymous tip came in so early this morning since it means I got to meet you."

"Anonymous tip?" she repeated.

"According to the caller, the hotel is in possession of a package addressed to our victim, Ms. Delia Sinclair."

"We are?" She looked over her shoulder at the office door like it was about to explode.

"That's what we've been told," he confirmed. "Would you mind checking for us? If the caller's information is correct, that package needs to be logged into evidence. If you find anything, try not to touch it. Just let me know if it's there and I'll come back to get it."

Now she looked scared out of her mind. "Can you come back and look for it with me? I'd hate to accidentally mess anything up for your case."

"Of course I will," he agreed, smirking my way as he rounded the counter and followed her into the office. A couple minutes later, they returned. Her face had lost all its color but Brody looked triumphant. For good reason, too.

"You have a spare evidence bag with you?" he asked, holding up an envelope in his gloved hands.

I played along with him. "We've got plenty in the car."

"Thanks for all your help, sugar. We better go bag and tag this to ensure the proper chain of evidence."

"Okay." Her voice held none of the warmth from earlier, most likely because this was as close as she'd ever come to violence in her life.

"Don't you think you laid it on a little thick back there?" I muttered as we walked away.

"It worked, didn't it?"

I couldn't disagree with his logic. "That it did."

The mission was successful. We had a new lead to follow and only two people had seen us enter and exit the hotel. "You going to turn the security cameras back on?"

"As soon as we get back to the suite."

"Delia was right," I murmured.

"She sure as shit was. I figured our trip was bound to be a wild goose chase. You could have knocked me over when I found this back there." Brody waved the envelope around. "You want me to open it?"

"Not yet," I answered, even though I was beyond curious to know what was inside. "We wouldn't have found it without Delia's help. It's only fair she's with us when we open it."

"Whatever you say," he mumbled. "I guess I'll just squeeze in some shut eye 'til we get there."

****

"Did you find anything?" Delia asked as she jumped up from the couch and ran toward me.

"Shockingly enough, we did," Brody confirmed.

"Really?" She looked as surprised as I felt when Brody walked out with the envelope. "What is it?"

"Don't know yet," Brody grumbled. "Saint said we had to wait until we got back here to open it."

"You did?" She stretched up on her toes to kiss my cheek.

"I did," I answered, trapping her against my body so I could repay her kiss with one of my own. Not to her cheek, though. I needed a taste of her plump lips since I hadn't been able to get one this morning. She had been sound asleep when we'd left and I didn't want to wake her when she needed the rest. By the time I lifted my lips from her mouth, her eyes were glassy, her lips were swollen, and we were both breathing hard.

"You guys look pretty busy, but I was kind of wondering...are either of you dying to know what's in the envelope or is it just me?" Brody's voice drew my attention away from Delia. The smirk on his face told me all I needed to know. I had never been one for public displays of affection, but it wasn't because I was embarrassed. I hadn't needed to worry about making any woman happy outside of bed since I never bothered with relationships.

137

My kissing Delia wasn't due to concern for her feelings, though. I was driven by my need to lay claim to her, something my best friend had apparently figured out. And based on his expression, he was amused by how differently I was acting with Delia. The craziest part was I didn't give a damn—not about Brody wanting to laugh his ass off at me or that being around Delia made me act like a completely different guy. I was quickly becoming addicted to the way she made me feel.

"Me," she whispered, her voice husky with desire.

"I guess we'd better open it. I'd hate to leave you wanting. For anything." I felt her slight shiver at my words before she stepped away.

Brody whistled lowly under his breath, raising his eyebrows as he shot me a look over Delia's head. "What?" I asked, trying my best to sound innocent.

"You know what," he mumbled quietly after Delia moved into the living room.

"Hand it over," I ordered, holding my hand out for the envelope.

"Denial isn't just a river in Egypt." He just couldn't resist the verbal jab before he gave me the envelope.

"Fuck you, too," I whispered as I walked past him.

I joined Delia on the couch, sitting close and pulling her into my side. "Let's see what Serena was hiding in here."

Sliding my finger under the flap, I tore the envelope open and dumped the contents into my hand. There wasn't much inside, just a business card with a post-it note wrapped around it.

"That's it?" Delia's voice held disappointment.

I peeled the post-it note back and realized the business card wasn't as ordinary as it appeared. The logo for TAG was innocuous enough, but nothing on the card explained what type of business they were. There was no address listed. No phone number. Just an odd website address with a username and password.

"Something's off with this," I said, handing the card over to Brody.

"Off? Delia repeated. "It's just a business card. What does the note say?"

I glanced down at the post-it and recognized Serena's handwriting. It was a note she'd written before secreting the business card away. And it was addressed to me.

Blaine – I didn't get far into this website before Jon called me and told me to run. Not sure how he knew I'd logged on. I'm afraid they'll find me and I want you to have this just in case. Thanks for coming to my rescue. Don't blame yourself if you were too late.

"Shit," I hissed, my jaw clenching as I used all of my training to hold myself still. What I really wanted to do was jump up from the couch and punch a hole in the wall. I knew Brody wouldn't give a damn and I could easily pay to fix any damage, but Delia was here and I didn't want to scare her with the depth of my anger at the sight of Serena's words.

"She's right, you know," Delia whispered, her hand running up and down my back. "You can't blame yourself for what happened to her. If anything, it sounds like her boyfriend is to blame and he's already paid for his mistakes with his life."

"Fucking A," Brody breathed. "Mistake isn't the right word for the kind of shit he was into."

When he turned his laptop screen our way, the website for TAG was pulled up. The mystery of what the company's initials stood for was immediately solved by the header on the screen: The Armory Group.

"Her boyfriend was an arms dealer?" My words came out as a question even though I knew the answer.

"Not the kind who does business with the Department of Defense. This site is on the deep web. If I hadn't had the URL or login information, even I would have had a hard time finding it and hacking in. I'm surprised they haven't deactivated the username by now, though."

"Maybe they kept it open while they were looking for Serena and thought it wasn't urgent any longer once they killed her," I suggested.

"Could be," Brody agreed.

"Serena's note said her boyfriend called when she logged onto the site," Delia reminded me. "Does that mean they have some way of tracking everyone who gets into the site? Are we in danger?"

"They may know I logged in, but there's no way for them to trace my location. I'm using a dynamic IP address and bouncing it all over the world," Brody answered. "Which will piss off their computer guy. It might even be enough to tempt him to leave the access active longer than he should so he can get another crack at me."

"You're sure?" I asked.

"Since when do you doubt my computer skills?" Brody's voice was filled with indignation, and understandably so. I never questioned him when he was behind the keyboard. Our lives had depended on his skills many times in the past and I'd never given it a second thought. Not until Delia's life also depended on them.

"Sorry, man," I apologized, my eyes sliding to Delia before I locked gazes with Brody.

His slight nod let me know he understood. "No worries."

Delia reached out and grabbed my hand. "I don't understand. He sold guns online? In some kind of black market or something? Wouldn't that make it easier for him to get caught?"

"It's more common than you think. Have you ever wondered why the deep web is also called the dark web? It's because there's a ton of black market transactions that happen there," Brody explained.

"Can't the police or FBI do something about it?"

"They try their best, but the authorities have no way of indexing the sites like they do with the ones stored on the surface web. They're putting a lot of effort into the fight with their cyber divisions, though."

"You'd be the one to know, wouldn't you?" The guy who had arrested him before he joined the Navy eventually went to work for the FBI Cyber Crime division. I knew Brody had kept tabs on the guy, in part due to curiosity, but also out of hurt pride. The guy had managed to catch him when he thought he was untouchable.

"I might sound naïve, but I had no idea stuff like this happened," Delia whispered. "I mean, I knew there were ways for people to buy guns when they weren't supposed to. Not from any kind of personal experience, though. Just from watching the news."

Brody and I had too much personal experience with illegal gun dealers. "There are three types of weapons purchases—the black ones, which are illegal, the white ones with all the paperwork, and the grey ones, which are somewhere in between."

"What type do you think Serena's boyfriend did?" Delia asked.

"Based on the level of security on this website, I would have to say black. As illegal as can be with the types of weapons they're offering," Brody answered. "I'd love to know how they managed to get their hands on some of this shit. They've got Soviet tanks, unmanned aircrafts, and helos on here."

"With inventory like that, Jonathan had to have been running with a serious crowd. Heavy hitters. He wasn't your run of the mill gun trader selling from the back of his car." It was hard to believe Serena had gotten mixed up with a guy like that.

"Serena had the card," Delia pointed out. "But, from her note, it sounded like she didn't know what kind of business her boyfriend was in."

Brody picked up the card and flicked it with his finger. "If she already knew, there wouldn't have been any reason for her to use the information to log into the website."

"She could have just asked him about it. Instead, she waited until he was out of town and logged in," I said, continuing where he left off.

"From work," Delia added. "You said he called her on her office line. It has to be the call she mentioned in the note. If I knew my boyfriend was doing something illegal, there's no way I'd ever risk my job by looking into it at work."

"She might have felt more safe doing it somewhere public, but it would have made more sense to go to a library or something."

"I think you're right," Brody agreed. "Odds are good she was curious about the card. Maybe she felt like something was off with her boyfriend and decided to do a little digging."

"It makes sense to me. They were in a relationship and he was keeping secrets from her. I might have even done the same thing in her shoes," Delia mused.

"She had no way of knowing the series of events she was about to trigger."

"Just enough to know she was in trouble and ask for your help," Brody added.

"If only I'd made it here in time."

Delia squeezed my hand again before resting her head on my shoulder. "It doesn't do any good wallowing on the 'what ifs'. You got here as quickly as you could and now you're doing everything you can to try to catch the guys who killed her."

"I will catch them," I vowed. I didn't have any other choice. It didn't matter if her note told me it wasn't my fault or how often Delia insisted I wasn't to blame, I felt guilty for not getting here sooner.

"What's our next step?"

"Your next step is to go take a nap while Brody and I work on a few things to see how much information we can get about TAG. Brody will do his thing on the computer while I make some calls. We have enough military and ex-military contacts. Someone is bound to have heard of them before."

"But I want to help, too!" Somehow, she managed to look both adorable and sexy while she pouted up at me.

"You can help me best by giving us some room to work while I know you're getting more rest."

"I'm not tired, though," she insisted.

I trailed my finger underneath one of her eyes before doing the same to the other side. "These tell me a different story. You've been through a lot the last couple days. Give your body what it needs to heal. For me," I added when she looked like she was about to argue again.

My softly spoken words were enough to get her to agree, albeit grudgingly. "Fine, I'll try to take a nap. But if I'm not asleep in the next hour, I'm coming back out here and you're going to find a real way for me to help. I'm pretty good with research."

"You've got a deal."

I was staring at the door after she closed it behind her, worried about the situation I'd brought her in to. If this arms operation was as big as the website indicated, keeping her safe was going to be harder than I thought. Especially since they were probably looking for her already, thinking she was Serena.

CHAPTER 12

Delia

How was it possible I did it again? I had been so darn certain there was no way I'd fall back asleep. When Blaine agreed to let me help after I laid down for an hour, I was thrilled. I even watched the clock as I lay in bed, counting the minutes until I could walk back out there and prove him wrong. Maybe I shouldn't have taken another pain pill because sometime after the forty-five-minute mark, I must have fallen asleep. And for a long time, since it was already lunchtime.

I rolled out of bed and sat on the side, letting my legs dangle over the mattress while I tried to get my bearings. My head was fuzzy after sleeping so deeply. I didn't even think I could call it a nap. It was more like passing out. I even had indentations on my cheek from the pillowcase.

Blaine opened the door slowly and peeked inside. "Hey, sleepyhead."

I rubbed at my face, hoping to smooth out the creases. Then I realized I probably had a serious case of bedhead. Seeing him stand there, the closest thing to a sex god I've ever seen in my life, while I was certain I looked like crap, pretty much sucked. I sifted my fingers through my hair, hoping I could make myself look semi-decent. As he shut the door and moved toward the bed, I fiddled with the shirt I was wearing—his shirt, the same one I'd had on for more than twenty-four hours.

"I need more shirts," I complained.

His eyes heated as his gaze dropped to my chest. "I'll run out and buy you some."

"I'm perfectly capable of buying my own shirts."

He reached out and traced along my collarbone, eventually pushing the shirt to the side. "I'm sure you are, but I like seeing you in mine. If I buy them, they're my shirts. Otherwise, I'd just call Brody and ask him to grab you some while he's out."

"But they won't smell like you," I admitted, blushing when I realized how much what I'd said revealed about my feelings for him.

He lifted his shirt over his head and climbed into bed next to me. "That's easily solved. If you smell like me, then my shirt will carry our scent when you wear it."

"You're awfully good at solving problems."

"I've got all sorts of *skills* you haven't seen yet." His voice held a sexual undertone I couldn't miss. Though, it wasn't blatantly obvious, which was far more intriguing—especially when I knew firsthand that when he used all of his considerable skills on a woman, she was putty in his hands. It was nearly impossible to be immune to his confident charm. I had already entrusted him with my safety and my body, but if I wasn't careful, he just might pose a threat to my heart.

"You holding out on me?" I shifted on the mattress, trying to get closer. The heat from his body chased away the cobwebs as my nap-induced fog slowly

146

subsided. My sleepiness had worn off, replaced by my desire. A desire which was well-timed since he just said Brody was gone. Wriggling my legs, my breath caught as I felt his hard cock pressed against my stomach. Knowing he was turned on only fueled my need further.

"If I am, it's for your own good. But someday soon, you won't need the pain pills. You'll be clear-headed enough to know exactly what you're doing."

"You feel so good," I whispered, rubbing against him in an effort to get even closer. I moaned helplessly when I felt his cock slide against my panties, my eyes drifting shut at the incredible feeling.

Blaine rolled me onto my back, moving over me before pressing his body down on mine. I was trapped beneath him. "Hold still, Delia. I can't take advantage of you like this."

My eyes popped open at the snap in his voice. The look on his face was one I'd dreamed of seeing directed my way—one I'd written about but never actually seen. His eyes were like blue flames as his lust blazed from them. His cheekbones were tinted red and his nostrils flared. His hungry look was raw and animalist—lust in its purest form.

My life was spinning out of control and there was only one thing I knew for sure right now. I wanted him. No, it was more than just wanting—I needed him. He made me feel safe. Wanted. Needed. "You want me."

"Not like this," he answered with a strangled laugh. "Later on, when you know what you're doing, if you still want this—"

I pressed a finger against his firm lips, stopping him from saying anything else. "I know exactly what I'm doing and who I'm doing it with, Blaine."

He dropped his head, resting it against my forehead as he held my gaze. "I don't want you to hate me later," he murmured against my lips.

Sliding my hands up his chest, I felt the beating of his heart and knew he wanted this just as much as I did. If I hadn't been falling for him before now, this would have made me start. He was so damn noble. I parted my legs, wrapping them around his hips until he was nestled between my thighs. His cock rested against my pussy, only the damp material of my panties and his jeans between us.

"I won't," I promised. "I could never hate you."

"Delia," he sighed, his breath caressing my lips before his mouth captured mine. His tongue swept inside, stroking mine. Slanting his head, he took the kiss deeper, growling into my mouth and sucking my tongue.

When his cock nudged at my entrance, I felt like I might die if he didn't take me right then. "Please."

My pleading finally seemed to break Blaine's control. Unzipping and shoving his jeans down, his cock sprang free. He held still for one moment, his eyes locked with mine before he pushed my panties to the side and thrust his hips forward, sliding his cock deep into me.

"So good," he moaned, his voice raspy with need. "I knew once I got into your pussy I was never going to want to leave again."

"Then don't," I whispered.

"Be careful what you offer me, Delia. I might take you up on it," he warned.

He began to move inside me, slowly pumping his hips, his cock nudging my cervix before pulling out again. This was unlike anything I had ever felt before. His eyes held mine, boring deep into my soul. I felt stripped bare, but I wasn't alone. It was shining from his eyes—Blaine was feeling as much as I was.

"More," I groaned against his lips.

Blaine reached down and pulled my thighs wider so his cock could go even deeper. I wrapped my legs higher around his waist, needing him to keep thrusting. "Fuck yeah, sweetheart. Let me give you more."

As we moved together, the tension inside me built higher. Blaine powered into me, harder and deeper. Stroking over that spot inside me with each thrust, driving me wild.

"Blaine!" I screamed as my pussy clenched around his cock, my orgasm exploding inside me.

My body shuddering beneath his, Blaine thrust deep a few more times before following me into his own orgasm—his hot come spurting inside me. "Fuck, baby," he hissed. "I took you bare."

My heart was already beating wildly, my chest heaving as I tried to drag air into my lungs. I wiggled in his arms, shifting my hips, and he slid out of me. "I'm on the pill," I blurted. "And I'm clean. It's been longer than I care to admit since I slept with someone."

"I'm clean, too. They tested me when I was in the hospital after my last mission."

"How long ago was that?" I cringed a little at my own question. Blaine was hot enough to draw female attention wherever he went. Plus he was a former Navy SEAL. When I'd been researching them for a book idea, I learned being a SEAL was like catnip to women. I had no doubt women threw themselves at Blaine. And often.

"Since I was tested? Fifteen months ago."

My shocked eyes jerked up to stare at him. "Really?"

"I was on a mission for a few months before then, so it's been closer to a year and a half for me."

His answer astounded me. I found it hard to believe he'd abstained for almost as long I had. "You were in the hospital?"

"Knee replacement." He cocked his left leg up and ran his knee along the outside of my thigh. "Took a bullet to the knee. Shattered it beyond recognition."

I leaned to the side to look down at his leg, tracing a finger along the scar. "Was that why you left the Navy?"

"Yeah, they gave me a medical separation. The joint replacement made me unfit for duty." I could hear the pain in his voice.

"Was it a difficult recovery?"

He tucked my head against his chest, his voice a deep rumble as I listened to him talk. "It wasn't easy, but I was lucky. Brody's brother made sure I had the best medical care available. He flew a world-renowned orthopedic surgeon overseas and made sure he was granted privileges at the naval hospital so he'd be available for any surgeries Brody or I needed. Then, when we got stateside, he arranged for around the clock care: physical therapists, a nurse, and occupational therapist. He even hired a personal trainer. Plus I had access to a swimming pool and hot tub. It was better than the best rehab facility the military would have been able to provide."

"How long did it take?"

"A few months before I was walking comfortably without assistance, but it still isn't back to normal. The doctor said it can take up to two years until the scar tissue heals and I'm able to build my muscles back up. I'll never be in the same shape again, though."

"I like the shape you're in now," I whispered, running my hand down his chest.

"Not as much as I like your shape." He thrust his hips upwards, still rock hard. "How's your arm holding up?

"Good," I breathed.

"The bruises?"

I swiveled my hips. "What bruises?"

"Sounds like now is as good a time as any to show you more of my skills."

****

Sex with Blaine was better than any sleeping pill. It put me right back to sleep and I woke up smiling. My arm felt better, too. He might have been right about rest being the best medicine. Although, the sex probably helped also.

I was lying on his broad chest, my ear resting against it while I listened to his heartbeat.

One, one thousand.

Two, one thousand.

Three, one thousand.

I counted each thump in his chest. It was steady and slow, under sixty beats per minute. I could almost believe it was a machine except it had been beating wildly when I landed against his chest after our second round of sex.

"I can hear you thinking." His voice was husky, a hoarse rumble.

"I thought your best friend was the one with a keen sense of hearing?"

He tilted my head until I was staring into his eyes. "It's a skill that seems to only work with you."

I blushed as I remembered how our earlier talk of his skills had ended up with him buried deep inside me. "Lucky me."

"I think I'm the lucky one."

"How's that?" I was lying in bed with a man who was sexy as hell and he'd just dedicated himself to making me come. I had no doubt who the lucky one was—and it wasn't him.

"I found you."

His words were simple, but they sent butterflies soaring in my stomach. I cupped his jaw, enjoying the feel of his hot skin under my hand. "I'm so glad you did."

"So fucking sexy," he murmured before dropping a quick kiss on my lips. "Which is why it pains me to say we need to get up."

"I have a better idea," I whispered against his mouth. "How about we stay in bed and I show *you* some of *my* skills?"

"I'd love to take you up on that offer, but Brody is going to be back any minute and I don't think you want him to find us still in bed." His smirk was knowing...and sexy.

"We'd have more time if you asked him to stop and buy me some more button-down shirts," I huffed.

His finger traced my bottom lip. "You've even got a sexy pout."

"I'm not pouting," I denied, knowing darn well I really was.

"If any man is going to buy clothes to cover up that hot little body of yours, it's going to be me." His voice was a growl. "You can wear one of my sweatshirts if your arm hurts too much to put on something of yours. Mine is bigger and should be easier to maneuver."

"Sounds good to me. I need to take another shower, too." After two rounds of sex, I definitely needed to clean up.

"Let me take a look at your stitches. It's been just long enough that you might be able to get them wet in the shower as long as you dry them completely off when you get out."

Blaine led me into the bathroom and I flipped the lid down on the toilet seat so I could sit. I held my arm out and he gently lifted the tape from my skin and peeled away the gauze. Twisting my arm so I could see the damage, I was surprised by how good it looked. "It's better than I thought it would be."

"Yeah, the wound is healing nicely," he agreed. "You should be fine to shower without covering it up. Just don't put your arm directly under the stream of water and pat it dry as soon as you get out."

"Will do." My tone was sassy, and I followed up my reply with a quick salute.

"Admit it," he growled. "You like it when I'm bossy."

"Maybe I do in bed, but we're not in bed right now, so march yourself out of here sailor. I'd like to get cleaned up before Brody gets back. I'm sure I missed a ton while I was sleeping and you're going to fill me in as soon as I'm done in here."

I wagged my finger at him and he nipped at the tip. "Yes, ma'am."

CHAPTER 13

Blaine

Walking away from Delia when I knew she was about to be naked and wet in the shower was one of the hardest things I'd done in a long time. I'd just taken her twice, but I was still sporting a hard-on from the vision in my brain of water sluicing down her bare skin. Getting it up had never been a problem for me, but she made me feel like a teenager again—only with the hardest hard-on I could ever remember having.

Control. In the teams, I was the guy known for always having it. When I needed it now, control was nowhere in sight. I knew Delia was to blame. She had the ability to make it slip from my hands in the blink of an eye. With her, I had very little self-control—pretty much none if I was perfectly honest with myself—and it scared the shit out of me.

"Sleeping beauty still in bed?" Brody asked as he walked in the door.

"In the shower," I bit out, pissed he came back early when I knew she had wanted to be done before he returned. Even more so because I damn well knew he was thinking the same thing I had been, even though he had to use his imagination to picture her naked while I knew exactly what she looked like.

When his eyes cut to the bedroom door, I wanted to punch him in the face. "I'm surprised you managed to pull yourself away from her."

I wasn't about to admit how hard it had been to leave Delia. "I knew I needed to be out here when you got back, so here I am."

"Right." His answer was a long drawl, which clearly said he knew I was bullshitting him, but he wasn't going to call me out on it—at least, not directly.

"Since when have you ever known me not to do what needed to be done?"

His gaze flicked back to the closed door again. "Since never, but this situation is different than the ops we were sent out to complete."

"What we're doing might not be sanctioned by anyone, but it's a mission just the same," I argued.

"You aren't exactly acting mission ready, Blaine. You positive you want to pursue this?"

"I can't let this go, Hack," I growled in frustration. "Serena meant something to me."

"I get where you're coming from. She's the first girl you put your dick into."

"Fuck you," I cursed, not appreciating his choice of words. "We grew up together. Our moms are friends. There's more to this than the fact that I had sex with her way back when."

"But have you really thought about what you're doing here? What you're risking?" he asked.

"She might not be one of my men, but it feels like I'm leaving her behind if I don't do something about what happened to her."

"Serena's already dead, Blaine," he reminded me. "Are you willing to risk Delia over this? Because I see it when you look at her."

"See what?"

"You're different with her. Softer. Hell, you bend for her like I've never seen you do with anyone else. You told me yourself, you didn't want her to go with you to Serena's office but you let her because she asked. You hated the idea of pretending to be cops when we went to the hotel until she was on board with it. You were always the guy who never bends. Hell, you're the one who drilled the only people we're supposed to be lenient with into my head," he muttered.

"Pets and babies," I finished

"We both know she's neither of those," he continued. "She's very much a woman. And I'm telling you now, Serena might have been your first, but you look at Delia like you want her to be your last."

"I've only known her for a couple days," I mumbled, even though I knew it wasn't much of a defense.

"Are you lying to me or yourself? You and I both know relationships aren't measured by how long you've known the other person. How many days did it take for us to become best friends?" he argued.

"That's not a fair comparison," I argued. "It's not like you and I met under normal circumstances."

"The same could be said for how you met Delia," he persisted. "Maybe it's not as extreme as hell week was, but the way you two met was still intense. Don't even try to sit there and tell me you don't know her."

"Fine," I admitted. "She's different. Amazing even."

"And that's exactly why you need to get her out of here. I get why you didn't let her go to the police at first, but using her as bait is a bad idea. There are too many ways it can go sideways. If you're lucky, she'll just end up pissed at you. But if things go to hell, she could be dead...or worse."

"Bait?" Delia repeated.

When I turned, I found her standing in the doorway. Brody and I had been so focused on our conversation, I hadn't heard her footsteps in the hallway. I wasn't sure how much she had overheard, but I figured it was enough based on how her arms were wrapped protectively around her stomach, tears streaming unchecked down her cheeks. Her eyes were filled with hurt and betrayal, and it was my fault. I had caused that look. There was no doubt in my mind.

I took a step toward her, but stopped when she shrunk away from me. Brody moved toward her, placing a blanket around her shoulders and leading her to the couch. It took all my control not to rip her away from him. She needed help and it killed me to know she wasn't willing to accept it from me right now. I needed to keep myself locked down and under control. I had to try to handle the situation like I had all the missions I'd been on: with the same cool, calm, and collected outlook I was famous for having. The only problem was there wasn't anything cool about the way Delia made me feel.

"I'm going to hit the shower, give you guys some privacy to talk this out."

My gut clenched when Delia's hand whipped out to grab Brody's arm. "Don't go. Not yet."

He sat down next to her and flung his arm around her shoulder, pulling her into his side. "There's a reason Blaine is called Saint. He's a good guy. I knew it when I met him and he proved it time and time again over the years, right up to the day he risked his life to save mine and didn't even get pissed when his time in the SEALs ended early because his knee was shot to hell carrying my ass outta the line of fire."

Delia's startled eyes flicked to me and moved quickly back to her lap. "He didn't mention that part of the story when he told me why he left the Navy."

"He wouldn't. Blaine's not the kind of guy to trade against the things he's done for his country or the people he cares about. He'd protect them with his life, doing it gladly and quietly without expecting anything in return," he explained, his voice gentling as he continued. "Like I know he would for you."

She jerked a little as he finished. "You really think so?"

"I know it for a fact."

I waited as Delia considered what Brody had told her, hoping she'd give me a chance to explain. It felt like my entire future hung in the balance. I knew I was getting ahead of myself, but I could too easily imagine having her by my side every day. In my bed each night. I didn't want to lose my chance with her because of a decision I'd made before I knew what she could come to mean to me. One which all my training told me was the right choice to make at the time. A decision I couldn't possibly regret. If I hadn't made it, I never would have had the chance to get to know Delia.

"Then I guess maybe I should hear him out." Her voice was soft and her cheeks wet, but the tears had stopped falling.

Brody squeezed her shoulders before standing and moving away from the couch. As he walked past me, he practically shoved me toward the spot he'd just vacated. "Take as long as you guys need."

I waited until the bedroom door closed behind him to sit down next to Delia. Taking her hands in mine, I placed a kiss on her palm before she jerked them away. When I heard the shower turn on, I knew it was safe to talk without Brody listening in. "I'm not sure how much you heard, but I swear I can explain."

Her arms were crossed in front of her body, fingers gripping the blanket tightly. "I walked in as Brody was telling you how bad of an idea it is to use me as bait because it might end up getting me killed."

"I wouldn't risk you like that," I swore.

"Can you sit there, look me in the eye, and tell me you weren't going to use me as bait?" The pain in her eyes was clear as day and it had nothing to do with her arm. What she'd overheard had obviously hit her hard. I needed to explain this so she understood how things had changed and when.

"Yes, absolutely," I insisted.

"How?" she cried. "I heard what you guys were saying and it sounded like Brody was trying to talk you out of the idea. Is that why? Did it take your best friend pointing out what a shitty thing that would be for you to see how wrong you were?"

I grabbed her hands, gripping them tightly in my own when she tried to pull away. "I'm not going to lie to you, baby."

"It feels like that's all you've been doing," she muttered.

Seeing her vulnerable like this caused something to tighten inside my belly. I'd hurt her. "The night we met, when I talked you into coming with me instead of calling the police, it was mainly because I thought there might be a way for me to use you."

Her body jerked, as if my words were a physical blow. "You didn't even know me. Why? How could you think about using me like that? Who gave you the power to decide whether I should risk my life?"

"My training taught me to look at people as chess pieces. To distance myself and see the strategic advantage they offered," I tried to explain, afraid it would be impossible for her to understand. "My missions always came first."

"Where do people fit into the equation?"

"The team came second and everyone else was last," I answered. "It was drilled into our heads, over and over again. Mission. Team. Individuals."

"You're not a SEAL anymore!" she cried. "And I deserve better than to come last to the man I'm sleeping with."

"I'd already decided well before we ended up in bed together that there wasn't a chance in hell I'd ever use you as bait."

Her eyes jerked to mine again, hope warring with disbelief. "When?"

"The second you placed your lips over mine," I admitted. "Hell, probably even before then since I fought you so hard on coming with me to Serena's office. I just didn't realize it until now."

"That's right," she whispered. "If you'd wanted to use me as bait, you would have been the one pushing for me to go. Not the other way around."

"My need to protect you superseded my training. I couldn't look at you as a pawn. Not when you're my queen—the most powerful piece on the board."

"My dad loves chess. I'm horrible at it, even after all the times he's tried to teach me how to play. I might not have been terribly interested, but I did learn a thing or two. Doesn't the queen protect the king? Even as a sacrifice sometimes?" Her head tilted toward me, her body not nearly as stiff as it had been when I first sat down.

"Not with us. In this game, *I* protect *you*. And if anyone needs to make a sacrifice, it damn well will be me," I promised. "Never you. Not when I'm here to stand between you and danger."

"Oh, Blaine," she sighed, tears welling in her eyes again. "Do you really mean it?"

"More than anything."

The moment she leaned toward me, I knew she believed me. Her hands released the blanket she'd been holding as she reached out for me. "It hurt so much to think you'd slept with me knowing you might have to use me. Or even worse—that you did it so you could make sure I'd be willing to do whatever you'd ask of me later."

"Fuck," I hissed. "Don't ever think anything like that ever again. I fucked you because I couldn't control myself. I should have waited until this was all over before taking you, or at least until you had a clearer head. I've never had any problem making decisions based on what I should do. Not until I met you."

Her voice was muffled against my shirt as I cradled her against my chest, happy as fuck to have her in my arms again. "It goes both ways, you know."

"What does?"

Although her cheeks were still wet, her eyes were filled with happiness when she looked up at me. "I'm pretty sure if it had been anybody else in my house that night, I would have never agreed to wait before calling the police. I certainly wouldn't have offered to share my bed. You're a game changer for me, too."

"Thank fuck," I sighed.

She nestled her head against me again and we sat there for God only knows how long before Brody came back out to join us.

"You guys work everything out?"

"Yeah, but I want to make sure this is clear. There's been a mission change," I said. "Delia's safety takes priority over figuring this shit out."

"Glad to hear you managed to pull your head out of your ass."

"You were wrong about what I was struggling with," I growled. "It didn't even take a day before I knew I couldn't use her that way."

"Then what the hell was that all about?"

"Me trying to decide whether I could call in the police and walk away completely," I admitted.

"For her?"

"For me?"

Their questions were asked simultaneously and both were said in the same shocked tone.

"Yeah."

"Man down," Brody whispered. "Never thought I'd see the day when a woman brought you to your knees."

I didn't think I'd ever see it either.

CHAPTER 14

Delia

An embarrassed giggle bubbled out of me, a complete surprise considering how upset I'd just been. I couldn't help it, though. As soon as Brody said 'knees', all I could think about was Blaine's order the first time we were in bed together. Then my thoughts shifted to an image of Blaine on his knees, his mouth on me. My core convulsed at the picture in my head and it was all I could do not to moan aloud—until I looked up and caught Brody's knowing gaze.

The last few days had been crazy, but the last couple hours felt like a roller coaster ride, complete with the highs and lows. Although low didn't seem like a strong enough word considering how devastated I felt knowing Blaine had thought about using me. It was hard for me to understand his perspective, but I'd never been in a position where I needed to look at people the way he'd been trained to do. And I couldn't exactly argue with his point of view. It had probably saved his life more times than I ever wanted to think about.

I believed him when he said he'd stand between me and danger. The conviction in his voice and the determination in his gaze left no room for doubt. It was enough to take the sting of hurt feelings away. I wasn't going to hold something he'd thought before he really knew me against him—certainly not when he changed his mind about it in less than twenty-four hours.

"You'll have to tell me later what made you blush this time," Blaine whispered in my ear.

"The key word in that sentence is later," Brody chimed in. "Right now, I need to fill you in on what I discovered while I was out."

I held up a hand. "Whoa! Before we learn the new stuff, you guys need to fill me in on what you learned while I was asleep."

"You haven't briefed her yet?" Brody asked.

I giggled again, my mind still in the gutter, thinking about Blaine pushing my panties aside before driving into me. I was pretty sure it wasn't the kind of briefing Brody meant.

"Not yet." Blaine's voice was filled with humor. When I looked up at him, his eyes were crinkled at the corners and his lips were tilted at the edges. He had an idea of where my mind had traveled to this time.

"She blush like that all the time?"

"She's sitting right here and doesn't like to be talked about as though she isn't," I muttered.

"Then try not to be so cute." Brody's retort had Blaine growling. Literally growling from deep in his throat. Then my stomach seemed to take its cue from him.

"Why don't you guys fill me in while I make something to eat? I'm starving."

"I could eat, too," Brody answered.

Blaine's arms tightened around me for a moment before dropping a quick kiss on the top of my head and standing up, pulling me to my feet. "You can always eat."

I walked into the kitchen while I listened to them tease each other.

"You calling me fat?"

Brody's frame was muscular, but he wasn't stocky by any means of the imagination. Neither was Blaine. To my eyes, they both seemed incredibly fit, although Brody's muscles were leaner. More sinewy. "Nah, we both know you've got another twenty pounds to go until you catch back up to me."

I popped my head out of the fridge so they could hear my question. "Catch back up to you?"

"Brody's injuries from our last mission were more serious than mine," Blaine explained.

My eyes jerked to the scar on his cheek. None of the photos the newspapers had run about him showed any such imperfection. Based on what Blaine had said about the quality of the medical care Brody's brother had gotten for him, I knew his injuries had to have been brutal if the plastic surgeons hadn't been able to fix his scarring. I was pretty sure I had detected a slight limp when he walked, too. "But you're okay now?"

"Better than I've been in a long time." Brody's voice held none of the humor I'd quickly grown accustomed to hearing from him. He seemed like an easygoing guy, but now I had to wonder if still waters ran deep. Maybe he used humor as a disguise so people wouldn't dig beneath the surface to see the real guy inside.

"I'm glad to hear it." I shot him a reassuring smile before dragging a bunch of stuff out of the fridge. "Sandwiches okay with you two? I'm too hungry to wait for anything else."

167

"Works for me," Brody mumbled before he popped open one of the containers and shoved a grape into his mouth.

"Why do I have the feeling you would have had the same answer no matter what I said we should eat?"

"Because you're right," Blaine answered.

"Not if it was sushi," Brody disagreed. "Or tuna casserole."

Blaine grabbed some plates from the cabinet and stacked them on the counter. "Correction. He would have said yes to anything you wanted to make as long as it didn't include fish."

"Are you allergic?" I asked Brody.

"Nope." His lips made a popping sound at the end, right before he tossed another grape into his mouth.

"He's never liked fish," Blaine explained. "Which made one of our missions interesting because we were in a small seaside town where it was a staple."

"Damn, I don't think I've ever eaten so many MREs in my life," Brody chuckled.

I'd run across MREs during my research. They were a meal ready to eat, packaged in a waterproof bag with a flameless heater. Sounded ingenious because they were easy to store and transport, but from what I'd read, they also tasted horrible. It was hard to imagine anyone picking an MRE over a real meal, even if they didn't like whatever else they could get their hands on at the time. "No MREs for you today. I've got everything I need to make club sandwiches."

"Thank God. I need something good. Just thinking about it brought back the taste of the jambalaya. Trust me when I tell you that whoever came up with that recipe needs to check their taste buds to see if they're still operational. I can't remember ever tasting anything more revolting, not even sushi."

"Enough about the MREs. What I want to know is will these club sandwiches have toasted bread?" Blaine asked.

I laughed as I pulled the toaster closer to the edge of the counter so I could reach it more easily. "Is there any other way to make them?"

He moved closer to me and wrapped his arms around my body. "Double decker ones?" His breath was warm in my ear.

"Yes," I sighed.

"With bacon and mayo?"

I turned in his arms to look up at him. "If by mayo you mean Miracle Whip, then yes. If not, then I think we have a problem here."

"A problem?" he chuckled.

"Yeah, I'm not sure I can be involved with a guy whose taste buds are so lacking he actually prefers mayonnaise to Miracle Whip."

Brody's laughter rang in my ears. "Dude, you're so busted. But hey, on the bright side, I'm not a fan of mayo. Maybe it's a sign you're meant to be with me instead of him."

"Shut the fuck up," Blaine growled at his best friend. "I can learn to like Miracle Whip, but I'll never stand for the idea of you with my woman."

"Your woman?" I repeated.

He leaned over and took my mouth in a deep kiss. Tongues tangled together, mouths slanted for better access, teeth nipping my bottom. There wasn't any other way to describe his kiss than what it was: a claiming. By the time he pulled away, my heart was racing, my legs were shaking, and my panties were wet. If he'd been trying to use a kiss to prove his point, he'd done a damn fine job of it.

"Mine."

"Yours."

Brody tossed a grape at us and I watched as it bounced off Blaine's head and fell to the floor. "If you're done proving your masculinity, I could really use something other than grapes to eat over here. I don't want to wither away."

"I did promise the man a sandwich," I murmured.

"Make mine bigger than his."

I knew Blaine was talking about his sandwich but my brain still managed to turn it into something dirty—again. My mind seemed to be stuck permanently in the gutter around him. I giggled as I answered, "I can do that."

"Tease," he whispered against my lips before kissing me one last time and then moving away. "Make me my sandwich, woman."

He followed up his order with a gentle swat on my butt, making me jump. "Hey!" I yelped. "Enough of that or yours won't be a double decker like mine and Brody's."

"That's just mean," he grumbled.

"No, please. Irritate the hell out of her. Please. It means more food for me." Brody rubbed his hands together in anticipation.

"You know club sandwiches are my favorite, dickhead."

I smiled at the coincidence. "Mine, too. Luckily, we have the easy bacon that just needs to be reheated in the microwave so they'll be done soon. Why don't you guys start filling me in on what you've learned?"

It was like my question flipped a switch in both men. The atmosphere in the room shifted as the smiles were wiped from their faces. Their expressions turned stony, the gleam in their eyes changed from playful to serious. They even stood taller than they had a moment before. I was seeing a glimpse of the operators they used to be when they served as SEALs.

"Go ahead. Give her the full sitrep," Blaine instructed Brody. "I'll fill in the blanks as needed."

"Per some secured files I accessed this morning, The Armory Group is already on the FBI and ATF's radars. Homeland Security, too. They've been hard to pin down because they conduct all their business on the dark web, and they're careful about the clients they accept. If you don't fit their criteria, you don't get access to their website. They keep their shit locked down tight. And by tight, I mean tighter than a nun's cunt."

The knife I'd been using to cut the sandwiches fell from my hand, clattering as it hit the floor. "Crap."

"Dammit, Brody! Watch your mouth around Delia," Blaine growled before turning to me. "You okay, baby? The knife didn't get your foot, did it?"

"I'm fine, and Brody doesn't have to watch his mouth around me. I've heard worse. I just don't think I've ever heard that saying before."

"Sorry," Brody said softly. I was surprised to find a blush creeping up his cheeks. "I forgot I was in mixed company for a minute there."

171

"I'm sure you've said worse. Blaine, too. No harm, no foul. Carry on," I insisted.

"Based on their setup, they have a damn good programmer on board. They tried to tag me when I logged in both times. If I were just about anyone else, they would have been able to trace me already. The bad news is I'm not sure how many more logins I can get away with until they're successful."

I slid a plate filled with a couple sandwiches along the counter to each of them. "That doesn't sound good."

"It's not," Blaine confirmed. "Which is why Brody went to run some errands. He needed some equipment he didn't bring with him. Stuff to help him if he needs to access their system again, and some supplies to beef up our security here."

"I thought you said the hotel was secure?" I asked Blaine.

"It's better than most buildings in town, but we can improve upon what they've done to add extra protection. Depending on what happens, Brody and I may need to leave you here alone. The only way I'm willing to do that is if this suite is as secure as I can possibly make it."

"Won't the hotel mind?"

The look Blaine leveled me with was filled with determination. "I don't give a fuck. Not when we're talking about your safety. I'm responsible for it and it's not open for discussion. With anyone."

"Plus, it means I get to play with new toys," Brody added, breaking the tension. He had an amazing sense of timing. I'd been gearing up to let loose on

Blaine for his high-handedness. Instead, I was distracted by the shiny equipment he started pulling out of a bag he'd grabbed from the living room. He piled a steady stream of high-tech gadgets on the counter. I had no idea what they were capable of doing, but they were very expensive.

"How much did you spend? I'd like to cover the expenses since you're installing this stuff so I'll be safe."

Brody's expression was startled and his gaze slid over to Blaine. "It wasn't as expensive as you'd think. I have damn good connections in the tech world so I get what you might call a professional discount. Besides, we plan to take it all back to Vegas with us to beef up the security on Damian's suite."

"I should at least pay for part of it," I insisted.

Blaine shook his head. "I thought we went over this already. You're my woman. I'm responsible for your safety. This equipment will help me do that, which means I cover the cost."

His words were said with a finality, leaving no doubt he was unwilling to bend on this issue. I had more than enough on my plate to push this with him anyway. "Let me see if I have this straight. We're up against a group of arms dealers who have been able to evade the FBI, ATF, and Homeland Security for God only knows how long. They killed Serena's boyfriend when she logged onto their website. Then they went after her, beating her before they shot her in the head. When we started looking into them a couple days later and they saw me at her office, they shot me because they thought they'd killed the wrong woman. That Serena was the one looking into them. Except she's dead and I'm not her!"

My voice rose a little higher with each sentence until I was practically yelling. It was either that or crying, and I was all cried out from earlier.

"In a nutshell, yes," Blaine confirmed.

Hearing those four simple words felt like all the air was knocked out of me. "This is big," I whispered. "Bigger than big. It's huge. What in the world are we going to do? How can we possibly go up against something like this? I get that you both used to be Navy SEALs, but you're still only two men and this is way over my head. I'm not going to be any help at all."

"I think I might have an answer to that question," Brody answered. "As long as Blaine agrees with my idea."

"This cyber shit is your territory, my brother. What's your plan?"

"Delia's right. We can't take them on by ourselves. We need to pull somebody else in on this. Someone with the power to take these guys down. Someone like Agent Phillips."

"No way," Blaine bit out as his body froze. "You're not making that call, Hack. Not after you've broken God only knows how many laws getting your hands on this information. It's too much of a risk for you."

I didn't know who this Agent Phillips was, but it sounded like Blaine really hated the guy.

CHAPTER 15

Blaine

I never thought the day would come when Brody would volunteer to call that prick. Some would say I owed our friendship to him since we would never have met had he not arrested Brody, but I'd never be able to look at it that way. We both knew he still had a hard-on for Brody and he'd like nothing more than to have a reason to bust his ass again.

It was jealousy, pure and simple, for the easy life he thought my best friend had. Sure he'd grown up in the lap of luxury, but it hadn't been easy when his parents were murdered and the authorities never found the killers. Or when he'd finally pulled himself together and discovered an innate ability with computers, only to get caught hacking when he was trying to get to the bottom of what had happened to his parents.

Agent Phillips pushed the prosecutor hard on Brody's case. His arrest was a major coup for him, one he planned to maximize to push his career forward. If Damian hadn't pushed back, Brody would have ended up doing hard time. Instead, he wound up in the Navy, where he definitely didn't have an easy time during BUD/S training. And things sure as shit weren't easy for him on our last mission. It should have been enough for Agent Phillips to back off, but he'd made it clear he

175

was still keeping an eye on Brody's activities to this day.

"These guys are going to be hunting for Delia. The second they saw her at the real estate office, they would have gone back and retraced their steps. By now, they know the woman they killed was checked into the hotel under her name. They're not the type to back down until they find her. You and I both know it. We've seen their kind before and we both know how much destruction they're capable of wreaking."

"I know," I growled, frustrated. What he just said was one hundred percent true and it pissed me the hell off that Delia heard every word of it. She looked devastated by the information. "We need to call someone, just not him."

"He's heading up the team hunting these guys at the cyber division of the FBI," Brody added.

"There has to be another option. One that doesn't put you at risk," I insisted. "They aren't the only ones after this outfit. We could call the ATF or Homeland. Hell, there's bound to be an ex-SEAL working at either agency. Someone who will understand. Who will be on our side one hundred percent and offer you protection when they learn where we came up with the information we have."

"I get where you're coming from on this. Trust me when I tell you I appreciate it, brother. More than you can know. But the cyber division is the best fit for this battle. These guys have some serious technology backing them up. We have to fight fire with fire and Agent Phillips is our best bet," Brody argued.

I didn't want to see the logic in his argument. It went against everything inside me to bring in people who were a danger to my best friend. "You're one of the best goddamn hackers in the world. It's a skill you might have gotten by birth, but it's also one the Navy honed into a weapon. What the fuck do you think he can bring to the table that you can't do on your own?"

"Neither of us can deny he's damn good at his job," Brody pointed out. "If he wasn't, he never would have caught me. And that was before he had access to all the shit the cyber division has to offer. Technology I'd have to beg, borrow, steal, or hack my way into if I wanted to use it. With a quick phone call, he has access to it all. The access we need if we're going to take these guys down."

If Brody insisted we needed them to get the job done, then I had no choice but to believe him. Which meant I was stuck with a plan I hated. One where he was sticking his neck out for Delia and me and there wasn't a damn thing I could do about it. "We're gonna ride this bullet out together, brother. If they try to take you down, I'm going with you."

"I'm in this, too," Delia chimed in. "If this guy tries to pull any funny stuff, I know some journalists who would be interested to learn the FBI was willing to run with your information and then use it against you afterward. If the worst case scenario happens, I'll make sure it gets ugly for them in the press. It will be hard for them to press charges against you if it's bad PR for them. I bet you have all sorts of medals from your time in the Navy, right?"

"I earned a few," Brody admitted.

"Perfect. The public would eat this story up. The decorated former SEAL wounded while serving his country, only to find himself the target of an investigation by an FBI agent with an axe to grind. How would it look if they went after you instead of being grateful for the help you provided to eliminate a threat on United States soil from arms dealers they haven't been able to catch on their own?"

She didn't give either of us a chance to answer before she continued. "I'll tell you exactly how it would look. Like arrogant, bumbling pricks."

The fierceness in Delia's voice and her determination to have my best friend's back was hot as hell. "Who knew my sweet girl could be such a badass?"

"I sure as shit didn't," Brody answered. "I never would have guess she was hiding that kind of fire underneath all that nice."

I'd seen the fire she was hiding inside. It came out whenever we argued and when we were in bed together. "She's got plenty of fire," I murmured. "I just didn't realize she had a little bit of SEAL in her, too."

They looked at each other and then back at me before they both busted up laughing. "Little," Brody gasped out.

"What the fuck's so funny?" I growled.

"I'm sure she'd like more than a little SEAL inside her," Brody joked.

Delia cracked up even harder. "There isn't anything little about him."

"Fucking A," I whispered as I realized exactly what I'd said and how they took it. "You're both perverts."

"It's not like you didn't know this about me already," Brody quipped.

Delia pointed to her blushing face. "I'm pretty sure you figured it out about me already, too. It's not like I can really hide it when I'm thinking something perverted."

"You make a good point," I conceded.

She smiled up at me and I was momentarily stunned by her beauty. I was damn lucky to find her and would do whatever it took to keep her safe. Even if it meant letting my best friend put his freedom on the line. "I know I'm at risk of you two taking this the wrong way, but it seems like the right thing to say. Let's do this thing."

I tried to make it a joke, but we all knew how serious this was. Brody simply looked at me and nodded his head. "I can make the call right now."

"You have his number?" Delia asked.

"I kept track of him just as much as he kept tabs on me," Brody admitted. "I knew about each promotion as he climbed the ranks of the FBI, some before he even did."

My best friend wasn't aware, but I'd kept my eye on the agent, too. I knew Brody didn't blame him for the arrest. He was young when he'd been arrested, but he understood the risks when he made the decision to hack into a government system in the first place. If anything, he blamed himself for not being good enough to avoid being caught. I respected his perspective on it, but I had no problem hating the guy enough for the both of us. If Agent Phillips hadn't been such an ass, I wouldn't have felt the need to make sure he stayed away from Brody. Knowing him as I did, it was going to take all the control I had to refrain from punching the guy in the face the moment I met him in person.

"I want you to record the call," I told Brody before he started dialing.

His finger hung over his phone as he looked up. "If I do, I might be adding another crime to the tally. I'm not sure what Georgia's rules are on wiretaps."

"I do," Delia piped in. "I had to research them for a book. You'll be happy to know you're currently in a state with a one-party consent law. As long as you consent to the conversation being recorded, it isn't illegal."

"Aren't you full of surprises today?" I asked, pulling her body flush against mine as we stood at the counter, watching Brody program his phone to record the call.

"I'm glad to be able to help instead of being a burden, even if it's by knowing something you guys could have looked up online."

"Hey," I whispered, tilting her head up so I could look into her eyes. "Don't ever say that about yourself again. You're not a burden at all."

Her gaze flicked over to Brody and then back again. "It feels like it. If you didn't have to worry about me, then maybe he wouldn't have to make this call. You'd have other options if I weren't in the middle of all this. You could even walk away because they wouldn't know to look for either of you."

"This isn't just about you, Delia," I reassured her. "They killed Serena. Even if you weren't involved, I'd still be here trying to bring them down."

"Plus, it isn't your fault you were dragged into this mess in the first place. That's on Serena. If anyone here is an innocent bystander, it's you. Blaine and I wouldn't be the men we are supposed to be if we let you go down for something that should never have been your problem to begin with," Brody added.

I felt her body relax as she let out a deep breath. "Okay."

"I want you to use speakerphone, too. I'll feel more comfortable if you have witnesses and a recording. Double protection if this becomes a clusterfuck later."

"You've got it," Brody agreed.

We listened as the call connected and rang on the other end.

Once.

Twice.

Three times before Agent Phillips picked up. "Brody Slater. I never thought my phone would ring and I'd find you calling me."

"You and me both," he replied. "But I seem to be in the middle of a situation which will be of interest to you."

"Really? Last I checked you were safely tucked away at your brother's hotel in Vegas, licking your wounds after you left the Navy."

He said it with such disdain, like Brody had been dishonorably discharged. This guy hadn't changed a bit. He was a serious asshole who still had it out for Brody, which meant we needed to be supremely

181

cautious with every step we took around him. Different day, same story as our other missions—*the only easy day was yesterday.*

"The Armory Group." Brody's reply was short and succinct, but it was enough to garner a reaction from Agent Phillips.

"What do you know about them?" His voice held none of the scorn from earlier.

"I can get you access to their site. URL, username, and password."

The silence on the other end of the line lasted long enough I began to think the call might have dropped. "Come again?"

"You heard me right the first time. If you want to catch TAG, then you need to come to Atlanta. I'm in the middle of a situation here and they're involved."

Agent Phillips chuckled. "You called me for help? Maybe I should look out the window to see if I can catch sight of any of the pigs that must be flying right about now."

"Too bad you aren't in hell already or you'd be able to see it frozen over," Brody muttered.

"Is that any way for a guy to talk when he's asking for a favor?"

"Bullshit," Brody hissed. "You can try to pretend all you'd like, but we both know you contacted your pilot to get the plane ready the second I mentioned TAG. I might need your help, but I'm also doing you a favor bringing you into this."

"You hacked into my computer?" he sounded shocked.

"No, I just know you well enough to guess how badly you want this collar," Brody explained. "It isn't exactly a leap of deduction to assume you'd want to get out here as quickly as possible if it meant you could be the one to lead the investigation resulting in getting them off the streets and finding out who's providing them with the big ticket items. It might even be enough to get you another promotion. Like my case did."

"Where can I find you when my team and I get into town?" His voice was back to all business, most likely because he didn't like Brody implying he'd be more interested in the case for a possible promotion.

Brody rattled off the address of the hotel and our suite number. "Call before you get here, though. Blaine and I are adding extra security measures tonight and I'd hate for you to set them off."

"I should have guessed you'd drag him into whatever mess you managed to find. All my research has shown him to be a stand-up guy, but if he isn't careful, he's going to end up beside you in a cell someday. It's too bad he got stuck with you in training."

I leaned over and hit the red button, disconnecting the call. "What a douche. I bet he'll be surprised to learn I'm the one who pulled you into this mess and not the other way around."

"Their visit should be loads of fun." Delia's voice was ripe with sarcasm. "What do we need to do before they get here?"

"Brody and I need to install the additional security measures. I want them up and running before Phillips and his team gets here. The last thing we need is for them to think they can waltz in and out of here whenever they'd like. The best way to demonstrate how serious we are about this suite being our safe haven is to make sure it has top-notch security."

"And make it painfully obvious they won't be able to thwart it easily," Brody added. "The thumb scan should take care of that, though."

"How can I help?"

If I had my way, she would help by allowing me to lock her in a failsafe room and not let her back out until this whole thing was over. It was never gonna happen, though. "You're good at research, right?"

"Very good."

"We need information on Phillips' team. Go online and gather everything you can find about them," I instructed.

"You've got it."

I watched her ass as she wandered away. She grabbed her laptop and settled on the couch while Brody and I got to work on making this place the fortress I wanted it to be come morning.

CHAPTER 16

Delia

"Will Brody be okay on the couch all night again?" I asked as Blaine joined me in bed.

The guys had spent hours installing the high-tech equipment and once they were done, they'd walked me through each of the new security measures to show me how they worked. The door to the suite wouldn't open unless Blaine, Brody, or I pressed our thumb against a security pad they'd added to the locking mechanism. Hidden sensors had been placed on the windows, wall, and door. Once activated, they would sound an alarm if anything crossed through their invisible beams. They'd also added a shatter-resistant film to all the windows. It was designed not only to keep the glass from breaking, but also to prevent people from being able to see inside our suite. Apparently, they thought it was necessary in case The Armory Group sent a sniper after me.

A sniper.

As if all these measures weren't enough, Brody had tapped into the hotel's security system so he could access their video feed and installed extra cameras of his own. We now had a bank of monitors in the living room showing us what was happening in the parking garage, valet stand, hotel lobby, in front of the elevators on our floor, the hallway in front of our room, and both stairways on either side of the building. I'd also heard Brody mumbling something about street cameras before I left the room. I wouldn't be surprised if he added some views overnight.

"Trust me, he'll be fine. Giving him the bed wouldn't do anyone any good. There isn't a chance in hell he'll get much sleep tonight. He'll be too busy fiddling with the equipment he let me install, making sure I didn't mess anything up. His addiction to energy drinks will keep him going until this is all over."

Nestled in his arms, I tilted my head to look into his eyes. "You've barely gotten any sleep either. What keeps you going?"

"You do."

My heart leaped at his stark admission. It was almost impossible to believe this amazing man was here in bed—with me. He'd point blank told me I was his woman, which had to mean he was my man. He was doing everything he could to keep me protected and I felt an urgent need to give back to him in the only way I could.

"Let me give you something to tide you over until tomorrow then." I rolled away from him to slide my panties down my legs before I got onto my knees and straddled his hips. Blaine hadn't bothered wearing his boxers tonight and I let myself sink slowly onto his cock. It took a moment for me to adjust to his size as he entered me. Even though he'd been deep inside me this morning, it still felt like the first time.

He lay underneath me, completely still. His hands clenched the sheets, knuckles white from how hard he was holding them. My breathing was fast as I stared down at him, impaled on his cock. The passion between us was incredibly intense and I wanted to enjoy every moment of being in control of our lovemaking.

I began to move slowly, sliding up and down while bracing my hands on his chest. I felt the rise and fall of his chest as he dragged air into his lungs. His heartbeat was much higher than when I'd counted the beats earlier. The pupils of his eyes expanded, his nostrils flared. He was so far removed from the steely operator I knew him to be. He more closely resembled a wild animal—one intent on claiming its mate.

I continued to move slowly, circling my hips on each downward thrust. His gaze lowered to stare at the sight of his cock disappearing inside my pussy.

"Lean forward," he whispered.

It was impossible to resist the snap of an order in his raspy tone. I bent down toward him, my hair spilling over my shoulders and brushing his cheeks.

"Closer." His tone was husky, the deep sound sending a quiver through my core.

When I swayed lower, the hardened tip of my nipple brushed against his lips. Opening his mouth, he clamped down on it, sucking deeply. My thighs trembled as he matched his pulls to my strokes. It wasn't long before I was panting, a sheen of sweat coating my skin. One that had more to do with the suckling of his mouth and the feel of his cock deeply embedded within me than my rhythmic motions. My core started to flutter around him as I hung on the razor-thin edge, so close to coming.

"Mine," he rasped as he lost control, releasing his grip on the sheets. His hands held my hips as he surged upwards, his hips grinding into me.

One of his hands slid up my back, pulling me closer, until my breasts crushed against his chest. He fucked up into me—hard. On his next thrust, his cock pushed all the way inside me, his balls slapping against my ass. My cries suddenly filled the room as my pussy contracted around him. Feeling my orgasm, Blaine didn't hold anything back. He slammed his cock into my pussy, over and over, going deeper each time. Finally, he was coming, the spurts from his cock lengthening my own orgasm until we were both trembling and motionless.

I felt boneless, my head nestled on his shoulder. His arms loosened and he ran his hands up and down my back.

"You okay, baby?"

"Mmm-hmm," I mumbled, unable to form actual words. I barely had the energy to breathe, yet Blaine was somehow still hard inside me—even after coming. How was that even possible?

"You feel so good," he whispered. "I can barely keep my hands off you, especially not when you're all soft and wet around me."

His hands slid lower, cupping my ass. Then his hips flexed as his hands pressed down, and I gasped at the invasion.

"That's right, baby. See how good it feels? I can slide in and out of you more easily." His hips moved while he spoke, his cock moving inside me with firm strokes. I was helpless, clinging to his shoulders as the speed of his thrusts increased.

Just a moment ago, I was certain I was beyond the ability to climax again. Now, it was steadily building inside me with each stroke of his cock, the heat suddenly burning out of control. I exploded, but Blaine wasn't done. He was relentless, slamming into me hard and fast.

Arousal was stamped on his face. His blue eyes glittering, locked intensely on mine. The muscles in his shoulders bunched as he moved my body up and down almost effortlessly. There was no escaping his powerful grip while he rammed in and out of me in a steady rhythm. The bed creaked with the force of his thrusts, but I was beyond caring who heard us. I'd stopped thinking about anything other than Blaine and the pleasure he was giving me.

Finally, when I started to think I couldn't possibly take any more, I felt him swell even larger. Then, with a hoarse cry, he erupted and his pulsing cock sparked another climax inside me.

"Holy shit," he whispered.

I collapsed on top of him, too tired to move another inch. He rolled me to the side, tucking his leg between mine as I felt the wetness trickling down my thighs. The last thing I remembered was the touch of his hand as he swept my tangled hair to the side. Then darkness claimed me as I passed out from sheer exhaustion.

****

I awoke the next morning to the soft swipe of a damp washcloth between my legs. My brain was still fuzzy and it took me a moment to realize what Blaine was doing. When I did, a blush swept across my skin. I'd climaxed more times than I could count and Blaine had come inside me twice. It was a sticky mess I should have cleaned up last night, but I'd been in no condition to do so. The thought hadn't even crossed my mind.

His laser focus was centered on my pussy. I watched, mesmerized as his tongue swept out to lick his bottom lip. I couldn't help but wonder if he was remembering the taste of me from our first night together. My eyes drifted lower, only to find his hard-on pressed against the zipper of his jeans. It wasn't surprising any longer since it seemed like a perpetual condition with him.

"Morning." My voice was hushed, but his gaze still jerked to my face. I didn't think it possible, but color crept up his cheeks as though he was embarrassed to be caught studying my pussy. I flashed him a warm smile to reassure him since I found it oddly arousing.

"I'd like nothing more than to climb back into bed with you," he murmured, "but Phillips and his team are going to be here in about half an hour."

"Half an hour?" I repeated, leaping from the bed. "Why didn't you wake me up sooner?"

"I was a selfish bastard last night, taking you twice when I should have let you sleep." His voice held remorse, but I didn't regret a single moment of our time last night. "You needed the extra couple hours this morning. There's no way to know how much sleep you'll be able to grab over the next few days."

I ran over to him and threw myself into his arms. "Don't ever apologize for giving me the most amazing orgasms of my life. I would gladly sacrifice sleep for a repeat of everything we did in that bed last night."

"I'll remember," he murmured against my lips. "Later, though. Right now, you need to get a move on so you'll be ready when they get here. I'd hate to have to shoot an FBI agent for seeing you half-dressed."

Had I not slid down his body to stand in front of him and found a gun in a holster hanging from his shoulder, I would have laughed at the idea. "You're armed."

Blaine's expression wiped clear at the shock in my tone, not seeming to like it. "I've been armed every day since we met, Delia."

"You have?" I gasped. "How could I have missed that?" I pointed my finger at his gun.

"You didn't miss it. I added the shoulder holster today," he explained. Then he bent over and pulled up the leg of his jeans to show me another holster holding a smaller gun strapped to his ankle. "And this one's hard to find unless you know to look for it."

"Holy crap," I breathed. "You've been walking around Atlanta with a gun strapped to your ankle this whole time?"

"Not the whole time, but I've had the .22 and my Ka-Bar on me whenever I've left the suite." He lifted the other leg of his jeans and there was a knife hidden there in a sheath. When he stood up again, he patted the gun at his side. "I feel better having my Sig on me, though. This baby set the gold standard by which all other combat handguns are measured. I've fired so many rounds from this gun, I can't even count them all, and it hasn't malfunctioned yet. No matter what the conditions are, if I have to pull it out of its holster, it's going to fire. When I get a chance to take you to the firing range, you'll have a Sig in your hand."

He was talking about his gun in the same tone most guys used to describe their car—or their mistress, if they had one. I was almost jealous until I heard him say something about taking me to the shooting range. I'd never seen a gun up close until now. Never held one. I had certainly never fired one. Heck, I'd never even thought about it, not even when I was writing books involving gunplay. Based on the steeliness of his gaze and the determination in his voice, it was something I was going to do sooner or later—whether I wanted to or not.

"C'mon, baby. Hop to it." He nudged me toward the bathroom door, giving my butt a swift pat for good measure. "You're still half asleep. Maybe the shower will help wake you up."

"Maybe."

I went through my morning ritual in a daze. Washing my hair, brushing my teeth, moisturizing my face. They were all things I'd done a million times before. If it had required any thought at all, I would have been doomed. Between all the mind-blowing sex, talk of guns like it was an everyday occurrence, and the FBI agents who were about to knock on our door, I didn't think I could handle anything else. When I'd wished for some extra excitement my last night at the cabin, I had no idea fate would take me seriously and land me in the middle of a situation better suited for the pages of one of my books.

I'd barely finished getting dressed when Blaine walked into the room. "You only have a few minutes. Brody said they just pulled up."

Apparently, the video monitors had already been put to good use. "All done."

"Come grab something to eat." His voice held the snap of authority.

"I'm not really hungry."

"Try anyway," he urged, leading me through the living room and into the kitchen. "Food and sleep are two necessities you can't afford to do without, especially not with the stress you're under right now."

"The stress is exactly why I'm not hungry," I complained. "I'm scared about what's going to happen with Brody and Agent Phillips."

"Don't worry about me." Facing the guy who had arrested him so many years ago didn't seem to faze Brody. He was finishing off a blueberry muffin and tossed one at Blaine, who peeled the wrapper back and handed it to me. "I figured this day would come eventually. I'm not thrilled to have to see Agent Phillips again, but at least we have an advantage since he wants this arrest to happen. Maybe even more than he wanted to get *me* back in the day."

"Then where the fuck are they?" Blaine asked. He broke a piece of the muffin off and held it to my lips before wandering over to the monitors. "Damn, it looks like they're going to stick close. Phillips has one of his lackeys at the registration desk."

193

"I'm pretty sure FBI agents prefer not to be called lackeys," I chided. "Seeing as they're highly trained professionals and all."

"Highly trained professionals my ass."

"Cut 'em some slack," Brody backed me up. "They sound like good agents from what Delia found last night. Plus, being stuck with Phillips for a boss has to suck for them."

"One thing's for sure, they're slow as shit since they just made it to the elevator," Blaine said.

I joined him at the monitor, waiting to see the agents come down the hallway. The bite of muffin I'd managed to choke down felt like it was crawling back up my throat. My heart was racing and my breathing shallow as I quietly freaked out, trying my hardest not to show it. A task at which I apparently failed miserably since Blaine moved in to comfort me.

"Calm down." Blaine's voice was firm, but his hand on my back was gentle.

"Calm down? Calm down, really? Here's a little tip. If you really want someone to calm down, don't actually tell them to calm down. It doesn't work. They don't calm down." The guys looked at me like I was crazy. They may have had a point since I was currently ranting like a lunatic. "Crap, sorry. Okay, I'm going to calm down. Here comes the calm. I will soon be calm. Maybe. Eventually."

Brody's eyes were wide when he turned to look at Blaine. "How many times do you think she can fit the word calm into the conversation?"

"I counted eight." Blaine's voice held dry humor.

"Gee, thanks, guys. Way to pick on the newbie."

They managed to distract me long enough that I must have missed the agents leaving the elevator and walking down the hall. There was a knock on the door and sure enough, a quick glance at the monitors showed the three agents.

"You good, brother?"

A quick nod of his head was Brody's only response. Blaine wrapped an arm around my shoulder, pulling me closer to his side as Brody walked over to the door. I took a deep breath in an effort to calm my nerves.

"We've got this covered. It'll be okay," Blaine whispered into my ear.

"Damn straight it will be," Brody agreed right before he opened the door. He didn't offer a greeting of any kind to the agents. Instead, he simply stepped to the side and let them walk past before shutting the door behind him with a thud.

My research of the cyber division showed a much larger team than what showed up today. Phillips had only brought two of his agents to Atlanta with him. Stuart Michaels was supposed to be his best cyber expert, with an extensive information technology background. Basically, he was one of their resident geeks—and he certainly looked the part with his thick glasses and slight build.

Cyan Steele was a different story altogether. She had a reputation for being a sharp investigator, but her background was in criminal justice, not computers. She would have made a perfect heroine in one of my books. She was about five-foot-ten with an athletic build, which still allowed for a few curves. The picture I hunted down last night didn't do her justice, though. In person, her face was striking. High cheekbones, striking green eyes, and plump lips framed by dark blonde hair. In the photo, it had been pulled back into a severe ponytail. It's amazing what a difference seeing it down made. One Brody seemed to notice based on the way his eyes followed her when she walked past him.

Introductions were made all around and the agents all stared at me oddly when Brody gave them my name last. He didn't offer an explanation for my role in all of this and I assumed they were trying to figure out what I was doing here. Their attention swiftly shifted to Blaine as he updated them on how he'd gotten involved in the situation and everything that had happened since he came to Atlanta.

"When this is over, am I going to find your TTP all over their system?"

"TTP?" I repeated, trying to stifle a nervous giggle at the image of toilet papering a house.

"It's a hacker's signature," Agent Steele explained. "Their tools, techniques, and procedures. They're our best bet to pinpoint the person or group responsible for a particular hack."

"I'm familiar with Brody's preferred methodologies," Phillips added. "If I find traces of his work in The Armory Group's network, I'll know he hacked the system. There won't be any way to hide it from me."

"You've got to be fucking shitting me," Blaine growled. "Are you seriously going to sit there and threaten Brody with an arrest after he called you in and is offering to serve TAG up to you on a silver platter?"

"My job isn't just about preventing harm to our national security. It's also to enforce federal laws as part of the nation's principal law enforcement agency." Phillips' voice could only be described as smarmy. I'd only been in his presence for a few minutes and I already understood why Blaine disliked him so much.

This time, it was me running my hand along Blaine's back in a soothing gesture. If this initial conversation was any indication of things to come, I didn't know how we were going to manage to work with them without someone getting shot. "We both know you look the other way when it gets you something you want more. The Armory Group is about as big as it gets. Back the fuck off Brody's ass unless you want me to show you the door."

"You won't show us the door," Phillips scoffed. "Not when you need our help. And you know it, too, or you wouldn't have called me in the first place."

"Maybe so, but we can just as easily pick up the phone and call in ATF or Homeland instead."

"That's enough, Saint," Brody interrupted. "I'm not worried. My access to TAG's site was done with a username and password they issued. We don't have time to argue over shit like this right now. Every minute wasted is another minute their cyber guy might decide to move the whole system, which means we lose access to their site. If he does, we're up shit creek without a fucking paddle."

Brody brought up something that had been bugging me. "They have to already know we've logged in again. Why haven't they moved it already?"

"It would raise red flags with their customers," Agent Michaels answered. "Moving their site would be the same as saying they've been compromised. There isn't any other good reason why you'd move a secure and untraceable site."

"Although they might know someone has been inside their system, they have no choice but to factor their customers into their risk assessment. The men running The Armory Group are dangerous but with the kind of weaponry they sell, their customers are bound to be even worse," Agent Steele added.

Brody moved his laptop to the kitchen counter, Agent Michaels trailing closely behind. "They probably still think it was Serena logging in again. At first glance, she wouldn't pose a major threat, but they have to be wondering why they haven't been able to trace her by now. Which means the clock is ticking and we don't know how much time we have left."

"I want that card," Phillips said, holding his hand out to Brody.

He handed it to him without mentioning we'd taken a photo of it earlier since the guys figured they'd have to fork it over right away. Phillips examined the card closely before giving it to Agent Michaels. "Verify the information still works."

Michaels flashed Brody an apologetic smile before powering up his laptop and using the information to log in. "I'm in, but it looks like they're already trying to trace my IP address." His fingers flew over his keyboard as he spoke. "And I'm out. Whoever their programmer is, he's damn good. I don't want to risk more time on his system until we've decided on a course of action."

"So, what's the plan, boss?" Agent Steele asked.

"The plan is simple," Agent Phillips answered, jerking his head in my direction. "Ms. Sinclair is going to contact them as Serena Taylor. She's going to offer them the card in exchange for her safety. She will also ask for a tidy sum of money. It will be easier for them to believe she's motivated by greed since it's why they're in business."

"The fuck you say!" Blaine roared, pulling me to the side. "These are incredibly dangerous men. They lurk in a world she cannot even begin to understand. There's no way I'm going to let you use her as a pawn. She's not expendable."

His use of the word pawn struck me like a punch in the stomach. I might not like Agent Phillips, but his plan wasn't any different than what Blaine had been considering when we first met. "Like you would have done before you got to know me?"

Chapter 17

Blaine

I searched Delia's eyes for any sign of lingering hurt feelings. When she tossed her question at me, I thought maybe it stemmed from a sense of betrayal we hadn't eliminated when we talked through what she'd heard me say to Brody. Now, I found myself hoping that was why she'd said it. I didn't like the stubborn tilt to her chin or how she stood taller, prouder—like she was determined to listen to what Phillips had to say regardless of how I felt about it.

"Blaine's right. Delia needs to stay as far away from this as possible. You have a woman with you," Brody said, jerking his head at Agent Steele, "if you really think your plan is best, use her as a decoy instead."

"It won't work," Agent Phillips insisted. "Open your eyes, man. Based on the photos you just showed me, she's a dead ringer for Serena Taylor. Same build and similar facial structure. Hell, someone at TAG already mistook her for Serena once, you told me so yourself."

"And then they shot her," I reminded him. "There's no fucking way I'm going to let her die for real because you're too goddamn lazy to come up with another plan. Your agents signed on for the risks, Delia didn't. She's the only innocent in this room. Do your damn job and protect her!"

"I'm not the one who pulled Ms. Sinclair into this and you know it," Agent Phillips retorted. "You guys are former Navy SEALs. You're supposed to be the best of the best for Christ's sake. You need to get into the game and use your head if we're going to have any hope of taking The Armory Group down."

"I'd happily step into Ms. Sinclair's shoes. Unfortunately, Agent Phillips is correct. That's not our best play here," Agent Steele added as she moved to stand next to Delia. "I may be a woman, but I lack the curves to pass as Serena. We could disguise my figure and maybe get away with it, but we'd still have the height issue to contend with. There isn't much we can do to make me look four or five inches shorter."

"Shit," I hissed. Seeing the two women standing side by side, I knew how ridiculous Brody's suggestion had been. It was something I should have realized instantly, but I was so far off my game, it wasn't remotely funny. If we moved forward with the plan Agent Phillips suggested, Delia was the only one who could pull it off. "Then we need a different plan. I'm not letting Delia close to these guys again. They executed Jonathan Roberts because Serena logged into their site. He was one of their own and they had no problem killing him. Then they beat the crap outta Serena before they shot her in the head, killing her. They already shot Delia once. She was lucky as hell their aim wasn't true or she'd be dead, too. I'm not going to serve them a golden opportunity to rectify their mistake."

Delia whirled to face me, her eyes lit with the same fire they held each time she argued with me. If anything, it burned brighter than ever before. "Excuse me? I'm standing right here. You don't need to speak for me when I'm more than capable of making my own decisions."

"Not in this," I bit out. "Your safety is my responsibility."

"How can you possibly keep me safe when they know I'm out there somewhere? I don't want to live the rest of my life looking over my shoulder, waiting for someone to come after me again. You know they won't let me walk away. It's why Brody called Agent Phillips in the first place. You both know the only way I'll ever be truly safe is if these guys are out of the picture. Completely."

"We're going to take them down," I insisted. "Just not this way."

She waved her hand at the agents. "They've been hunting these guys for God only knows how long, right? They haven't managed to catch them yet, and neither have any of the other agencies working on this case. A veritable alphabet soup of the best our criminal justice system has to offer hasn't been able to do a damn thing to get close to The Armory Group, but *I can* because of some sick cosmic joke. They say everyone has a twin out there and mine just happens to be a woman they'll hunt to the ends of the earth to make sure they can keep their damn secrets. Well, I say we don't make them look too hard. Let's turn the tables on them and use the only advantage we have right now— *me.*"

Delia was chomping at the bit to do something, anything, to get her life back. I understood why she felt this way, but I didn't like it. Not for her. Not for the woman who was so sweet, she could almost give me a toothache.

I'd busted my ass for years defending God and country. I already paid my dues with blood, sweat, and tears. My sacrifices weren't going to be in vain, dammit. There's no chance in hell my woman was going to be in the line of fire. Her dues had already been paid. By *me*.

She hadn't trained day in and out for years like Brody and I had. She didn't carry a badge like Phillips and his team. She spent her days safe and sound in her home writing stories with happy endings for fuck's sake. She wasn't prepared for the danger she'd face if she went along with Phillips' plan.

But I didn't know if I could talk her out of it. Gone was the soft woman I'd woken up to this morning, looking beautiful and warm as she lay curled up in bed. In her place was a Delia I hadn't faced yet. She looked fierce—still beautiful, but icy as she paced the room while Phillips outlined his plan.

A plan I wanted Delia to have no part in unless it was from the safety of this suite.

A plan she seemed eager to carry out.

A plan that terrified me—using her as bait to draw the people who had killed Serena into Phillips' web. Men who would be gunning for Delia the moment she was within their crosshairs.

My woman. Bait.

It had to be some sick cosmic joke. Payback for dragging her into this mess in the first place instead of sending her away to safety. I couldn't get it to compute in my brain. It was impossible when all I could think about was her getting shot—again. The Armory Group finishing off what they'd tried to do when they saw her at Serena's office. Her body riddled with bullets instead of the graze she'd taken to the arm.

I didn't like the plan.

I made it clear how much I didn't like the plan.

Clearly. Concisely. Often.

They just kept going through it, until they thought they had it all figured out. Like it was feasible. Only it wasn't because the whole damn thing rested on Delia's shoulders. We were a group of two former Navy SEALs, three FBI agents, and a civilian. *How the fuck was it that everyone thought the civilian, the only innocent in the room, was the person who should take point on this?*

My entire body tensed as Agent Phillips approached her. I didn't trust the bastard as far as I could throw him. I wanted nothing more than to drag her as far away from him as possible. It wasn't a viable option, though. If I tried to run with her and they caught up with us, Phillips would never let me be part of the takedown. There wasn't a chance in hell I was going to let Delia do this without me, so I found myself in the position of having to suck it up and deal without punching him in the face. He knew he had me between a rock and a hard place and had been taking full advantage of the fact as soon as he knew Delia was locked into the plan.

My decision not to punch him was about to fly out the window as I focused on what he was saying to her. "Beautiful and brave. It's quite the combination, Ms. Sinclair."

Yanking Delia away from him and placing her behind my back, I faced off with Phillips. "She's mine. You don't get close to her."

His chest puffed out like a fucking peacock thinking he could take me, the clueless bastard. "During this operation, she's my asset. I most certainly will need to get close to her to prep her for what to expect. Very close since she's going to need to be wired."

"I don't think you understand what I'm telling you," I growled. "Nobody gets close to her, and I'll kill to keep it that way. Not you. Not TAG. Nobody."

"Are you threatening me?" Phillips' voice climbed as he spoke. "I could throw the cuffs on you right now if I wanted to."

"How about we all calm down?" Agent Steele intervened. She slid a hand between us and pushed against my chest as Delia's hands pulled at my shoulders.

"Calm, huh? Delia was telling us all about being calm right before you guys got here." Brody's voice held a wealth of humor. It was a technique he'd used in the past to defuse tense situations. "Maybe we should ask her to go over her theory again?"

I felt her giggle before I actually heard it. The front of her body was pressed against my back and she was shaking from the effort it took to hold back her laughter. A battle she didn't win. Thank fuck, too. It was enough to stifle my anger.

"Maybe not," I said wryly as Delia slipped under my arm and settled at my side.

"Are you willing to move forward with the plan without Mr. West's assistance?" Agent Steele asked her.

"Absolutely not." Delia's response was quick, her voice firm. There was no hesitation.

"That's what I thought." Agent Steele's focus switched to her boss. "Alienating the two former SEALs your operational asset wants at her side would put this entire assignment at risk."

"It's not her choice who stays or goes. This is my operation."

Based on the way her fists clenched and her face tightened in anger, Phillips' response irritated Agent Steele almost as much as it did me. "She's a civilian. It's not her responsibility to face The Armory Group, but she's agreed to do it anyway. At great risk to herself, I might add. Do you really want to run the chance of losing her cooperation? I certainly don't. Nor would I want to be in your shoes when you'd have to explain that you were the reason she refused to help to the higher-ups in DC."

It was the smart approach to take with Phillips, reminding him of the powers that be in DC. He was hungry to move higher up in the ranks and he'd end up with a black mark in his file if he mishandled this operation. Agent Steele handled her boss like a pro, earning my respect. Brody's, too, if the approving glance he sent her way was any indication.

"I'm not the young man I was back when you arrested me, Phillips," Brody warned. "I won't need my brother to pull strings if you go against us on this. I've built my own contacts over the years. Blaine has, too.

We have an entire brotherhood behind us. There's no such thing as an ex-SEAL. Once you're in, you're in. And Blaine and I have the budweisers to prove we're in. Any idea you have of doing this without our participation, get it out of your head now."

"If your brotherhood is so strong, why did you have to call me for help?" Phillips was all bluster now. It was obvious from his expression that he knew it, too. He just wasn't willing to back down from the argument yet.

"Because it was the right thing to do," Delia answered, stepping forward to stand between Brody and Phillips. "And they're honorable men used to making tough decisions."

Agent Steele moved beside Delia. "C'mon, boss. Let this go before we find ourselves on the other side of that door with no way to get back inside. I, for one, don't want to be standing out there while the guys from ATF laugh their asses off as they waltz right past us and take over this operation."

Phillips studied Delia before shifting his gaze to Brody and finally moving on to me. "I understand this operation may be difficult for you due to the nature of your relationship with Ms. Sinclair. I'm even prepared to make some concessions because of this. However, we need to be clear on one thing. This is my operation. I'm in charge. Not Ms. Sinclair. Not Hack. And not you. Me."

The sneering way he used Brody's nickname pissed me off all over again. "I never said you weren't. As Delia already said, we called your team in because it was the right thing to do. We know you're our best bet to take these guys down and fast. The key word here being fast, so how about we get back to the task at hand."

"Good," he replied, satisfaction clear in his voice.

"Although, if you fuck this up, you'd better believe it won't just be Blaine and me you'll have to contend with. Damian will be after your head, too." It was so like Brody to help diffuse a situation only to stir the pot once everything had been settled. I didn't know anyone else who liked getting the last word more than he did.

"Enough," Agent Steele growled. "Let's go through the plan again. From the top. Start us off, Delia."

She nodded in agreement before moving to stand by Brody's laptop. "I'll log in to their website, go to the chat function Brody found the last time he was in their system, and send a message asking for a meet. I tell them it's none of my business what they're into. That I blame Jonathan for dragging me into this mess and I just want out of it. I'll promise to leave town. No calls to the police. No talking to anyone about anything to do with The Armory Group. I won't even go back to my apartment. I'll meet with them and hand over the card I found in Jonathan's apartment. The only thing I want in return is cash. Not because I'm blackmailing them, of course. It's so I can lay low and make sure I don't do anything to draw attention their way."

"How much will you need?" Steele asked.

Delia's reply was swift. "Not much. Just one-hundred thousand dollars."

"There's your first problem and she hasn't even met with them yet," I chimed in. "By now, they're familiar with Serena and her habits. They won't believe she only wants a hundred K to walk away from all this. With the way she liked to live, she'd ask for a helluva lot more than that."

Agent Steele looked toward Phillips, deferring to him for the first time since the argument. "He knew Ms. Taylor the best. We should increase the amount if he says it doesn't fit with her personality."

"TAG's operation is huge. They aren't your run of the mill gun dealer selling .22s from their trunk. They won't flinch from a big number. It might even make them take her more seriously. Greed is something they'll understand," Brody added.

"Ask for a million," Steele instructed Delia, who paled at the idea.

"Alrighty then, I'll just ask the arms dealers for a million dollars. Even though they want to kill me. Makes perfect sense to me."

"The important thing is to keep the chat going for as long as you can," Agent Michaels chimed in. "If their security is as good as Mr. Slater says it is, I'll need as much time as you can buy me to piggyback in and infiltrate their network."

"That's one of the parts I don't understand," Delia said.

"I'm going to be on the hunt for their customers' personal information. It will be their biggest bargaining chip during questioning. If I can get it before the arrest, we won't have to give them a deal."

Delia still looked confused. "I thought Brody said we needed to limit how much time we were logged in so they can't trace us."

"I did, but they won't be searching as hard because you're offering to meet them. Why bother when they think you'll be within their grasp soon?" Brody explained. "Your chat session is our perfect opportunity to hack their system. We'll be able to slide in with your login and dig around while they think you're busy setting up the meet."

Agent Michaels nodded his head. "It's like they handed us the keys to their kingdom. It doesn't matter how good their security is, we'll still be able to get in with you. The only question is, will we be able to stay in long enough to get what we need?"

"If not, Ms. Sinclair meeting with them will be even more vital to this operation," Phillips said. "We won't be able to let a single one of them get away. Not if we want to be able to access their site again to get what we need."

"No pressure or anything," Delia said wryly.

I listened as they went over the details of the meet. Where it would be. How many agents they'd call in for backup. Everything. I absorbed the details, burning them into my memory, unwilling to leave anything to chance. This might be Phillips' operation, but I was going to put stopgap measures into place. Fuck asking for permission. I could ask for forgiveness later.

CHAPTER 18

Delia

By the time the agents left, I was exhausted and beyond ready to head to bed. We'd spent the entire day and night working through all the details until they were drilled into my head. I'd picked at my lunch and dinner since my stomach was still unsettled. I didn't think I was going to be able to eat a real meal until this was all over. I'd been incredibly relieved when we'd finally headed into the bedroom. Until Blaine turned on me the instant the door closed behind us.

"You shouldn't have agreed to the plan."

I thought we'd worked through all of this when he'd finally agreed to move forward. He sat right next to me the whole time we ran through the plan, even offered suggestions here and there. Some of which Phillips had taken and some he'd adamantly refused to consider. Apparently, Blaine had just been waiting until we were alone to try to talk me out of this—again. "And wait for however long it would take for this situation to be handled?" I asked. "My parents are due to port in two days. I'm already going to have to explain the voicemail the police have no doubt left them. You know, the one about my murder? I don't want to have to follow that conversation up by them claiming I need to go into hiding for heaven only knows how long while

211

the FBI tries to apprehend the arms dealers who want me dead. Arms dealers who have a knack for technology and could probably hunt me down regardless of where I hid. Or the witness protection agency stashed me, if I even qualify for protection. Arms dealers who have successfully evaded authorities for years."

His lips tightened as he watched me rant and rave. "You done?"

"Yeah, I guess so," I gasped, out of breath—I'd just gone on and on without stopping for air.

"Good." He pulled my pants down my legs abruptly before lifting me and tossing me onto the bed. I landed on my back with my head sinking into one of the pillows at the headboard. One of his hands went to the shirt I was wearing and he yanked it open, sending buttons flying. My chest heaved as I tried to drag air into my lungs. His eyes latched onto my chest, my breasts spilling out over the open edges of the shirt.

"I think you need a reminder that you're mine," he growled.

He palmed my breasts, shoving them together before bending his head to claim a nipple with his mouth. He was rough, using his teeth and mouth to suckle me hard. I felt each tug deep in my womb. The edge of pain sparked a desperation I had never felt before. It was heightened by how vulnerable I felt underneath him in an open shirt and panties while he was still clothed.

He reached over to the nightstand, dug in the drawer, and grabbed a bottle of lube. A bottle I had no idea was even in there. I tensed, my butt clenching at the thought of him taking me there.

"I'm not ready for that," I whimpered.

His eyes blazed down at me as he tipped the bottle and poured some of the contents between my breasts. "Wasn't planning on taking your ass today," he murmured with a dark edge to his voice, letting me know it was something he planned on doing someday.

He used his hands to spread the lube across my chest, palming the curves of my breasts. My nipples pebbled as he massaged it into my skin. His hands swept across my skin in exquisite torture. My back arched for more as his hands left me to flick the button on his jeans and lower the zipper. He didn't bother to pull them off. Instead, he freed his cock and let his jeans hang from his hips. The sight of his hands captured my gaze as he stroked himself slowly from root to tip. By the time he was done, his cock was hard and glistening with a coating of lube.

A gasp slipped from my lips as he moved over me, straddling my stomach, completely in control of his heavy weight.

"That's right, sweetheart," he purred in approval. "Keep your mouth open for me just like that."

He squeezed my breasts together and pushed forward with his hips. As soon as his cock neared my lips, I tilted my head and drew him inside, desperate for the taste of him. When he drew back, I mewled in complaint, not ready to let go of his cock.

"More," I pleaded, grasping the firm muscles of his ass in an effort to bring him closer.

"You'll take what I give you," he growled, one hand reaching out to grip my hands and place them above my head.

He stayed still for a moment, holding me captive beneath him—my hands unable to move in his grasp and my eyes locked with his. I grew more desperate, until finally, he moved. His cock slid between my slick breasts and he let me suck him into my mouth at the end of each thrust. Over and over again, until I felt his legs trembling with the control he was barely holding on to.

"Blaine, please," I said softly. "I need you."

"Damn straight you need me. Don't you ever forget it," he groaned, his body tightening as his cock twitched. He levered himself up and fisted his cock, tugging once, twice, three times until his come spurted onto my breasts.

I lay there, wearing nothing except for the shirt hanging off my body, a pair of sopping wet pink panties, and his come painted across my chest. I had never been more turned on in my life.

"Blaine, please," I pleaded.

"I need to taste you," he growled, ripping my panties from my body. I trembled as his fingertips drifted up my thighs, spreading my legs and holding me firmly in place. My hips jerked as I felt the brush of his lips over my slit followed by a puff of hot air. I was twisting in his hold by the time he moved lower, tormenting me with flicks of his tongue along my pussy lips.

My hands gripped his head as I desperately tried to pull him closer. But I wasn't able to move him an inch. He just wouldn't budge. But he moved me. Oh God, did he move me. He nudged my legs higher before spreading me open with his fingers. My core clenched at the hot puff of air I felt right before his tongue flicked my clit. Gently at first, like he was lapping away at me. A low moan crept up my throat, and it seemed to be the sign he was waiting for. The pressure of his strokes increased, until I was writhing in need beneath me.

"More," I pleaded. His tongue felt amazing, but it wasn't enough to send me over the edge.

Finally, he slipped his fingers through my wet folds, sliding upwards first to pinch my clit with a hard squeeze. Pleasure, and a touch of pain, exploded through me.

"So wet." His voice was a low rasp against my flesh. One I felt almost more than heard.

"Please," I begged, needing his finger to slide lower.

Blaine knew exactly what I wanted, but he took his sweet time giving it to me. His finger swirled my clit and then slid lower, centimeter by painstaking centimeter, before it finally sunk inside me. A few deep strokes later, he added another finger and twirled them around, scissoring them and stretching me wide. I was already close and my walls clenched against his fingers, sucking them deeper. Another lick of his tongue over my clit was enough to send me over the edge. My hips surged up and I screamed out his name as waves of pleasure crashed over me.

He wasn't ready to go easy on me, though. He continued to pump his fingers over and over, making my orgasm go on and on, until my voice was hoarse from screaming and I was drenched with sweat. By the time he pulled his fingers out of me, I was shuddering and panting for air.

"What the heck was that?" I gasped.

"Me reminding you who the boss is in this relationship."

There was so much wrong with that statement. Beyond wrong even. I should have been pissed at him, but I knew it stemmed from him being forced to take a back seat with Agent Phillips—and even more so from being worried about my safety. It was hard to be angry when his frustration and anger was motivated by his need to keep me safe. Instead of taking him to task for his ridiculous statement, I decided to cut him some slack. "Does this count as makeup sex then?"

"You ain't seen nothin' yet, baby," he whispered against my lips, and it was the right decision to make. He then proceeded to demonstrate what all the fuss was about when it came to makeup sex.

****

The following morning came much too early for my liking. It wasn't because I didn't get enough sleep. It was because I was scared. Although I'd been the one to push for my participation in everything that was about to go down today, I didn't feel prepared for what was about to happen.

"I can hear those wheels turning in your head again." Blaine's raspy voice startled me since I didn't realize he was awake, too. Not that I was hard to startle—I was already feeling jumpy.

"Here I thought I was doing a good job of quietly freaking out," I half-joked. "But I made the mistake of forgetting about your ability to hear me thinking."

"It's a good thing, too. You don't need to freak out quietly. Not when I'm here. How can I make it better if you don't talk to me?"

"I'm not strong enough," I admitted. "What do you do when you're not strong enough?"

I knew my question wasn't fair. Blaine had tried to talk me out of this plan, yet here I was, expecting him to give me the strength to move forward.

"You act as if you are." His response was simple. Firm. Like it was easy to do. And maybe it was for men like Blaine. Men who'd been to hell and back. But it was daunting to me. "If that doesn't work, take your strength from me. I won't leave your side. Not for a minute."

The surge of relief I felt knowing this powerful man had my back was huge.

Incredibly humbling.

And life changing. As easily as I took my next breath, I knew I could happily spend the rest of my life with Blaine—and I hoped it lasted a lot longer than the next twelve hours. While my view of the world changed in an instant, he continued to talk, offering more reassurances that everything was going to be okay.

"We're going to take additional measures for your protection as well. Brody has a couple receivers he's putting into jewelry for you, a bracelet and a necklace you'll need to wear. He'll wait to activate them until after the meet begins in case they scan you. He's also putting beacons into anything you'll be wearing: shirt, belt, pants, and shoes."

It sounded like Brody had been busy last night. "What are the beacons for?"

"If they manage to separate us, Brody will be able to use it to track and rescue you."

"Brody and you," I corrected. "That's what you meant to say, right?"

"No, I said it right the first time. The only way we're going to be separated is if I go down. I can't enact a rescue if I'm in the hospital or dead."

He meant it.

He *really* meant it.

The only way Blaine was going to leave my side today was if he was physically unable to stay there. As much as I wanted to think about what his actions said about his feelings for me, now wasn't the time. One or both of us could be dead before the day ended. I only had this morning to prepare for what lay ahead. If something went wrong, it was more than likely going to be my fault. I was the weakest link. There was no denying it. The only thing I could do was listen to the people around me who knew what they were doing and depend on them to help me navigate the danger I found myself in.

"I think I'm ready for the first part of the plan. Agent Steele was clear about what I'm supposed to say during the chat. I'll do my best to lengthen the conversation. It's the actual meet that scares me."

Blaine pulled me into his arms, his chin resting on top of my head. "I'm not going to lie to you, I'd be relieved as fuck if you told me you wanted to back out of the meet. I know Phillips would blow a gasket, but you say the word and I'll have you out of here before he can do anything about it."

"I know you would, but I don't want to spend the rest of my life looking over my shoulder and never really living. Not when The Armory Group has already killed two people to cover their activities up. I won't build what little life I could have on the bodies they'll bury along the way, either." I shifted in his arms so I could look up at him. "I know you don't want me to do this, but I need your strength right now. Please help me do this."

He didn't look happy about it, but he did back down. "Whatever you need."

"Walk me through what to expect during the meet?" Agent Steele had done it several times last night, but I hoped Blaine's insight would help calm my nerves. Make me feel more prepared.

"When we get to the park, Phillips and his team will already be in place. So will the other agents he's called in. Brody won't be with them. He'll be waiting on a motorcycle. At the first sign of anything going wrong, he'll come in and get you out of there."

That wasn't part of the plan. It had to be another thing Blaine and Brody had cooked up on their own. "What about you? How will you get out?"

"If all hell breaks loose, the last thing you'll do is worry about me. You get your ass on the motorcycle and let Brody take care of you until I can make it back. There's no room for negotiation on this point."

"How can I just leave you there?" I argued.

"Easily," he answered. "I excel at escape and evasion tactics. Having you out of the way will make it easier for me to get out of there. With the location of the meet, the motorcycle is a necessity. A car isn't an option. If it had been, we would have gone that route because I don't want you more than an inch away from me. But I know Brody will get you out of there if I can't. He's the only other person in the world I'd trust with your life."

"Okay," I said quietly. "What else do I need to know?"

"When we go in, keep your eyes open, but don't look for the agents. You need to forget they even exist. If you do notice one of them, let your eyes drift past. And don't worry if you look nervous. I'm sure they expect you to be."

"Acting nervous is probably going to be the easiest part for me," I admitted.

"Phillips wants you to get them offering you the bribe on tape. Doing so will require us to talk to them. They're not going to be happy I'm there with you, but I'm betting they won't be surprised either. Not if they caught sight of me after they shot you," he explained. "One of the teams of agents will be casing the park, seeing if they came alone. Another team will be securing the perimeter. Brody will be listening in on their comms and talking to me through an earpiece so I'll be in the loop at all times. I don't trust Phillips to give me a heads up if something goes wrong. Not if it puts his operation in jeopardy. But I have one priority: you. And you've only got one job: do exactly what I tell you to do when I tell you to do it. Can you do that?" he asked.

"Yes," I answered.

"If I get the all clear sign from Brody, we'll play it the way Phillips wants us to and we'll try to get them on tape paying you the million dollars. If not, I'll give them very little time to neutralize the threat. They can't do it, we're outta there. The agents manage to hold up their end of the operation, we're outta there as soon as the takedown begins. And if things go sideways, you're outta there on the back of Brody's bike."

"So, what you're telling me is you're going to find a way to get me out of there."

His eyes narrowed. "This isn't a joke, Delia."

"I know it isn't, Blaine." I really didn't think it was a joke, but hearing him say "outta" so many times was slightly humorous.

"When I said my only priority was you, what I really should have said is getting you out of this alive is my only priority. I've worked out an exit strategy for every contingency I could think up. It's what I've been trained to do. I've never been happier to have been a SEAL as I am this morning. It means I have the skills to keep you safe from harm."

With that last sentence, I fell even harder for Blaine.

CHAPTER 19

Blaine

Walking Delia through the plan again this morning helped, but I still had a bad feeling about the meet. I knew the FBI would have the park wired and any spots they missed, Brody would have covered. I'd bet my life on his technical skills in the past without blinking. Now I was betting Delia's and it made me want to flinch.

She was a game changer for me, and everything depended on her. Gone was the nervous woman from this morning—she seemed more confident now, ready to face the danger inherent in this operation. Willing to risk her life to put a stop to The Armory Group. And chomping at the bit to put the first step of the plan into motion.

"Is it ready yet?" It wasn't the first time she'd pestered Agent Michaels and Brody while they were running their final checks to make sure they hadn't missed anything before she went online.

"What we're doing is a science, and science can't be rushed," Brody replied.

"Do you think he means they aren't done?" Delia turned toward me as she asked the question.

"No, we're done. I just wanted to yank your chain a little since you are worse than a little kid on a road trip asking his parents if they're there yet."

222

Delia whirled back around to glare at Brody. "I'm nervous, okay? The least you can do is cut me some slack."

"Any other day, I'd be happy to do that. Not today. Not when you need to chill the fuck out."

"You do realize 'chill the fuck out' is a ruder way to say 'calm down', right?" Delia sounded like she was about to dive into an argument with him. She would find a way to bicker about the color of the sky if she was in the mood to get into it.

"Baby, did you miss the part where he said it's done?"

Her head swiveled my way as her focus shifted back to me. "Crap! I totally missed that part. I guess it's time to do this thing."

Agent Michaels walked her through the steps one last time. Brody had turned the monitor so it was facing the kitchen cabinets, away from everyone else in the room. Phillips hadn't seen the need, but Michaels had backed Brody up when he insisted TAG would try to find a way to activate the webcam during the chat session. The last thing we needed was for them to catch sight of a bunch of federal agents. It would send them running in the blink of an eye.

I didn't even want them to see me. Delia was going to be on her own for this part. I wanted every advantage we could get going into the meet, and if they knew I was there, we'd lose the element of surprise when I showed up at her side. When Agent Michaels was done, I led her around the counter, whispering a few last reminders in her ear. "If anything feels off, disconnect the chat. I know you're supposed to keep them on as long as you can, but you need to trust your instincts. And if you see Brody or me giving you the signal, shut it down right away."

"Got it," she whispered back. We'd already discussed the agreed upon signal before the agents arrived. We picked one nearly impossible to miss: a swiping motion across our neck.

I tilted her chin up and stared into her beautiful face for a moment, burning the vision of her all lit up with fierce determination into my memory. "You've definitely got this."

Her smile was blinding, a sign I'd given her what she needed to settle any remaining nerves she had. As I moved away from her, Phillips cleared the suite. Only six of us remained—his team and mine. Phillips, Steele, and Michaels huddled around a laptop on the coffee table while I joined Brody near his. Each of us was silent while Delia logged into TAG's site. She waited a moment before clicking on the chat function, mindful of her directive to stay in their system as long as possible.

Brody's fingers flew over his keyboard and an image popped up on the monitor. I wasn't standing next to Delia, but I could see everything on her screen now that he'd synced with her. The first step of this stage was complete and I gave her a quick thumbs up, wanting her to know the connection had been successful on our end. It was one less thing for her to worry about.

We didn't have long to wait. They were quick to respond to her chat request—with an innocuous handle better suited for a normal retail site than an arms dealer on the deep web.

Customer Service: You're a hard woman to track down, Serena.

Delia: I was motivated to stay hidden. Getting shot isn't something I want to experience again.

Customer Service: You know what they say, curiosity killed the cat. Maybe you should have kept your nose out of our business.

Delia: I wish I had. More than you can possibly know.

Customer Service: It appears we're at an impasse. I'm assuming you had a reason to reach out to us?

Delia: Yes, I'd like to come to a mutually beneficial agreement. One where I'm out of the picture but still alive.

Customer Service: I'm listening.

Delia: We meet face to face. Today. I hand over the card. You let me walk away and you'll never see or hear from me again.

Customer Service: Sounds to me like the agreement you're proposing benefits you more than us. How do we know you'll keep up your end of the bargain?

Delia: How do I know you won't kill me the moment you see me?

Customer Service: Touché, Serena. Point well made.

Delia: I'm willing to leave Atlanta. For good. But I'll need funds to do it.

Customer Service: How much?

Delia: A million. In cash, small bills so they'll be harder to trace.

Customer Service: We could put a hit out on you for less than a million.

Delia: You'd have to find me first.

Customer Service: I'm sure we will eventually. Out of curiosity, what exactly would our money buy us with you?

Delia: The card with your login information, my laptop, and me living the quiet life as far away from your activities as possible.

Customer Service: People have been known to do stupid things when motivated by greed. How do I know you won't head straight to the police after we hand over the money?

Delia: Because I'll have exactly what I want already. My life and the money. If it makes you feel more comfortable, take some photos of me during the exchange. Then I'll never be able to go to the cops because you'll be able to incriminate me.

Customer Service: Point well made again, Serena. I'm beginning to think you were wasted on Jonathan.

Delia: No doubt about it. I was.

Customer Service: Okay, I'll bite. Let's meet in person. Do the exchange and go our separate ways. A shame really since you've peaked my interest.

Delia: Can you get the money together in two hours?

Customer Service: Easily.

I continued to switch my focus from the monitor to her face, making sure she was holding up okay under the pressure. As soon as Delia gave him the details of the location Phillips had selected for the meet, I caught sight of Brody out of the corner of my eye. He was giving her the signal to end the chat. She pressed the power button and held it down, as Brody had instructed her to do. She didn't hesitate, not even when Phillips stalked toward her.

"You were supposed to keep them online as long as possible," he growled before turning toward Agent Michaels. "Please tell me she didn't fuck this whole thing up because she got scared and decided to turn the goddamn computer off. Did you get what we needed?"

"I didn't." Phillips looked like he was about to blow a gasket. "But I think Mr. Slater might have had better luck than me."

Everyone's attention turned toward Brody, who was standing there with a smug grin on his face. He pulled a thumb drive out of his USB port and held it out to Phillips. "You know my skills. What do you think?"

Phillips snatched the drive from Brody and handed it over to Michaels. "Download it and make sure he didn't miss anything. Call the office and get everyone's help on this. I want eyes on all the data he managed to grab, and I want it now. We only have a couple hours before the meet. I need to know exactly where we stand evidence-wise before it happens."

****

"I'm nervous," I admitted, my voice low, not wanting Delia to hear me. The shock on Brody's face was clear

227

and unsurprising. We'd been on countless missions together. I'd never been nervous on an op before. I'd always been focused on the objective: get in, get the job done, and get out. I'd never felt apprehensive like this before.

"You want to back out? I can take the three of us so far off the grid, they'll never have a hope of finding us."

His voice was the barest hint of sound, but I knew he meant every word. Regardless of the sacrifices it would take to make us disappear, Brody would do it if I asked. Even at this late juncture when we'd have to make our escape literally under the noses of the dozens of federal agents. "The meet's set. They've seen her face through the webcam during that damn chat. We need to move forward and take these fuckers down. Eliminate the threat to Delia for good."

Delia had changed into the outfit Brody prepared for her—complete with two mics and a grand total of six tracking beacons. He'd managed to get an extra one into a ring, and fuck if it didn't piss me off to watch him hand it over to her even though it might save her life. I was an unreasonable bastard when it came to Delia. A bastard who needed to get his head in the game before he fucked up the operation and got them both killed. I wasn't willing to let that happen, not to Delia. And if I had my way, I'd make it through this alive, too. Then I'd get to work on convincing her to spend the rest of her life with me.

The three of us rode in the back of an FBI van to a location about a half mile out from the park. The plan was for Delia and me to use the car they'd provided to drive the rest of the way. All the additional agents

Phillips had brought in were already in place. One of their tech people, a woman, since I'd insisted on it, was checking the placement of the mic they'd put on Delia while Brody and I were standing a couple feet away. Phillips and Steele were on the other side of the van, just out of our line of vision. Michaels was inside, manning the monitors, where he'd stay for the remainder of the operation.

"I better head out." Brody's voice was a whisper of sound in my ear. I'd slid the earpiece he'd given me in as soon as I exited the van.

My eyes remained locked on Delia, but I nodded to let him know I'd heard.

"The bike's already in place, with a spare laptop and tablet waiting for me in the saddlebag. You won't be able to see me, but I'll have eyes on you the whole time. Anything seems off, I'll let you know. You won't be alone out there. I've got your back," he promised.

"Hers," I corrected. "Delia's safety is the objective here. She's the mission."

"It's the same as having your back. I know what she means to you and I'll protect her with my life," he swore.

"I hope it doesn't come to that."

He flashed me a quick smile. "Hoping's for pussies. SEALs don't need to hope. We just get the job done."

"All in. All the time." It was a familiar saying to both of us. One we lived during our training and every single mission.

"Hooyah!" It was the last thing he said before he slipped out of the parking lot, rounding the corner quickly so he could get into place before anyone noticed he was missing. The motorcycle was an exit strategy we hadn't shared with Phillips and his team. He had made his priorities clear, and they were different from mine. Arguing with him wouldn't do any good and I wasn't about to back down. Not with Delia's life on the line. I did what I thought was necessary to secure her safety. If Phillips ever found out, it would only be because we needed to use the measures Brody and I had put in place. And if it came down to that, he'd have more important shit to worry about than Delia's disappearing act.

Agent Steele's eyes locked with mine as she and Phillips walked toward me. Her gaze shifted over my shoulder for a moment, and I knew she had noticed Brody was gone. They both seemed to have an internal radar where the other was concerned. A quick nod was her only reaction. It was enough to tell me if her boss didn't realize Brody had left, she wasn't going to be the one to tell him—yet another reason to respect the female agent.

"I'm ready," Delia said as she joined us, stepping to my side and sliding her arm around my back.

"Do you need to go over the plan one last time?" Agent Steele asked.

Phillips didn't wait for Delia to answer. Instead, he tossed the car keys. "We don't have time to go over it again. She's not going in alone, for God's sake. West can baby step her through it if need be. Isn't that why they insisted he go in with her?"

We had insisted—Delia, Brody, and I. Phillips had wanted me to wait in the van, or better yet, the suite. He said he didn't want me interfering with his operation. The bastard had argued that the only way this would work was if they thought she was alone. A defenseless woman they'd already shot once. No visible threat so they would be less on guard, more apt to say something incriminating. Delia going in alone wasn't something I was willing to agree to. If they wanted her at the meet, the only way she was going was with me at her side. Period. End of story. Eventually, Phillips realized I wasn't going to back down and altered his plan to include me, but had Brody in the van—where he probably thought he was right now. *Clueless bastard.*

"We're good," I confirmed, leading Delia to the car and helping her inside. By the time I was in the driver's seat, both agents were headed to the park, hand in hand.

"I don't envy Cyan her role today. She's stuck playing happy couple with Phillips. Just the thought makes my skin crawl."

"Cyan?" I repeated, surprised to hear her refer to Agent Steele by her first name.

"She told me I earned the right to call her that. And I like her. She'd make a great heroine in one of my books."

"There's a lot to like about Agent Steele." It wasn't the usual way we'd done a comms check, but it would work. At least I knew Brody could hear everything being said in the car. Plus, his voice came through crystal clear in my ear.

"Brody likes her, too."

"I totally forgot he was listening in," she muttered. "Although, I could already tell he likes her. I think the feeling might be mutual."

I parked the car in an open spot across from the park. It was time to get serious. "Play time is over. We have to assume they have eyes on you from the moment you step out of the car. Wait for me to come around and open your door. Stay close to my side. Be ready to run or drop to the ground the moment I tell you to do it."

"Got it." All traces of humor had leeched from her voice and she didn't complain about the snap of authority in mine. Her eyes were focused and clear. She was as ready as she was going to be. I was damn proud of her for holding up like she was. Better than some of the sailors I'd seen in battle.

I exited the car, my eyes sweeping the park as I searched for open lines of fire and escape routes. Fuck, the bench Phillips had selected was a crap spot. It left Delia vulnerable to several locations where a sniper could have been put in place. There was no way in hell I was going to lead her there. Luckily, Brody was way ahead of me.

"Picnic table to the right, the one under the tree. It offers cover and it's one of the spots where I placed a camera and mic last night."

I scanned right and found the spot he was referring to instantly. It was a much better position and the only place in the park I was taking Delia for this meet.

She reached for my hand the moment I opened the door. As I helped her out of the car, I pulled her body close to mine and bent low so she could hear me without my voice being picked up by the microphones. I didn't want to give the agents a chance to claim the table and take it out of play. "Slight change of plan. Don't act surprised, but we're heading to a picnic table to the right. The spot Phillips wanted us to use isn't secure."

She handled the shift in strategy like a pro, allowing me to lead her in the opposite direction without any outward reaction. I got her settled at the table, her back to the tree for additional protection. Then I scanned the park, marked the location of each agent, and catalogued the appearance of anyone else. There were a couple guys playing Frisbee about thirty feet away on a hill who seemed out of place. The way they moved was too precise. Swiveling to face the direction where Brody was located, I moved my head in a virtually indecipherable jerk toward the guys. Brody was the only one who'd pick up on the motion, it was so slight. Years of training side by side and serving on countless missions together left us in sync in ways nobody else would understand.

"Looks like TAG brought in some backup." Brody's voice came through loud and clear. He'd caught the signal like I knew he would. "The woman with the golden retriever to your right. She's setting off my radar big time, too."

His instincts were good. When I casually turned in her direction, I caught her staring at Delia. As soon as she saw my eyes turn her way, she shifted her focus to her dog, but I saw the recognition in her eyes. She was an operator of some kind, and she wasn't ours.

"Contact is confirmed," he said quietly in my ear. "Black SUV parked next to the car you used. Two men, white. One's six-foot even, jeans, black t-shirt, blond hair. The other is five-foot-ten, khakis, blue dress shirt, brown hair."

His rundown allowed me to pick them out quickly as they headed our way. I moved to stand between Delia and their entry point. "The car is out of play. First dude dropped his sunglasses and it took him two minutes to retrieve them after he set down the black duffle he's carrying. Coincidentally, his glasses fell under your car."

I heard what he didn't say. There were only two reasons it would have taken the guy that long. He either placed a tracker on the car or wired it to blow. Black t-shirt was the muscle. Dress blue was most likely the guy Delia had spoken with online this morning—and the highest up the food chain we'd get with this meet. This was the guy Phillips wanted the most.

I leaned closer to Delia, speaking directly into her ear. "The car isn't a viable exit strategy for us. It's been tagged already. That leaves us with the feds, on foot, or Brody's bike. Nod your head once if you understand."

A quick jerk of her head was all the confirmation I needed. We were running out of time. "The two guys walking toward us, about fifty feet out, are the ones we're meeting. Chick to the right with the dog is likely an unfriendly. Two guys playing Frisbee might be with them as well. Whatever happens, do not engage with any of them."

By the time I got the last word out, we were no longer alone. Dress blue had joined us, his muscle standing slightly behind him and to the left. "You didn't mention you were bringing company along, Serena."

"Neither did you," I answered for her, drawing his attention right where I wanted it—on me.

"It's amazing how fickle women can be. Her boyfriend isn't even buried yet, but here she is with a replacement already. Are you sure you want to risk your life for the kind of woman who didn't even bother to properly mourn the man she was sleeping with for a year?" His tactic was a good one, divide and conquer. Insert a seed of doubt into my mind about her trustworthiness and maybe get me out of the picture voluntarily. "Or is it about the money for you? If so, I'm sure we can come to some kind of agreement."

My eyes shifted to the black duffle before locking with his. "I'd prefer to keep both, the woman and the money."

"What if I made you choose one or the other?" he asked.

"Not sure you're in a position to make me do anything, buddy." He might be smart, but he wasn't as good as he thought. I caught the look he gave the woman with the dog. "You're not the only one here who thought to bring backup."

Surprise flared in his eyes, followed by a hint of respect. "But did we both think to use a sniper? I know I did, which means you're not getting out of this park with her alive unless I allow it. I could just have him put a bullet through your head right now and then I'd be the one with the woman and the money."

235

It didn't matter how smart he was, I had several advantages over this guy. The main one being the tactical support Brody was able to provide. "Confirmed. There's a sniper on the building at your four o'clock. If needed, exit routes are still available before the feds can take him out of the picture. Best one on foot would be at your eight o'clock. The tree would provide cover. The bike's still an option, too."

I felt it then. The prickle at the back of my neck which told me things were about to go sideways. My gaze dropped to the black duffle and then trailed up the arm holding it. A million in small bills would have some weight to it, but his muscles weren't straining. Not even the slightest. They were not here to negotiate, hadn't even brought the damn money. I had no way of knowing what they had planned, but Dress Blue didn't look like he was in any rush, which meant he needed more time to get whatever he had up his sleeve set into motion. Time I couldn't let him have.

The plan to get evidence of a payoff on tape was out the window. It was unlikely I had additional time to give Phillips. As I turned to grab Delia's hand, I casually scratched my neck from side to side and then let my hand drop back down. "Goat fuck confirmed. Packing up my shit and starting the bike now. Repeat signal if you want me to come for Delia."

I didn't have time to consider my next step before the woman with the dog started to move closer, her hand sliding behind her back.

"Down! Now! Gun!" I felt the whoosh of air as Delia dropped to the ground behind me. "Under the table."

My gun was already out of its holster by the time she'd taken cover. I fired off two shots in quick succession. The first one took down the woman and the muscle went down with the second. Brody's voice was screaming in my ear as he relayed information to the feds who had subdued and arrested the Frisbee guys, taking them out of the equation. When the dust settled, it was just me and Blue Shirt standing face to face, our guns aimed at each other's heads.

"Looks like we have a Mexican standoff." This confirmed it. They guy was definitely not as good as he thought he was if he didn't realize it was the feds who'd taken down part of his team.

"That would only be true if I couldn't proceed or retreat without being exposed to danger."

He moved his hand from side to side. "You move and I shoot you. It's pretty much the definition of being exposed to danger."

"Except you didn't take into account the outside forces moving in on us." I didn't move my gun or shift my focus away from him. My situational awareness was good enough that I didn't need to. Instead, I waited for him to look around and take stock of the position he found himself in.

"Your team is down. They have your sniper in custody." The second part was a bluff since I hadn't gotten an update on the sniper yet, but he didn't know that. "The feds want you alive, but I'd actually prefer dead. Please, do me a favor and give me an excuse to blow your brains out."

"Who the hell are you?"

"She brought in the SEALs."

CHAPTER 20

Delia

It sounded like things happened so fast after I rolled under the picnic table at Blaine's command, but it also felt like everything moved in slow motion. I didn't know how else to describe it other than surreal. I tried to be as still as possible, my arms wrapped around my head as I cowered under the protective shelter, hearing two shots ring out. Blaine was out there, unprotected. Two instincts warred within me: one to stay hidden and safe and the other to look to make sure he was okay. Knowing which choice he'd want me to make, I stayed where he'd told me to go and waited it out. Finally, I heard him say he was a SEAL and I knew he was still alive.

Then I heard the sound of running feet and one of the agents reading someone their rights. Blaine's voice again as he answered some questions. At some point, Brody had joined them, too. The minutes passed painstakingly slowly, until it finally sounded like the action had died down.

"Can I come out now?" My voice came out wobbly and soft, but Blaine must have heard me. He was suddenly crouched down in front of me, holding his hand out.

"You okay, baby?" he asked, his gaze raking down my body, making sure I wasn't hurt.

"Yeah, I am. Are you?" My question was the barest whisper of sound as I caught sight of the body on the ground behind him. It was the guy who'd been holding the duffle bag with a bullet hole between his eyes.

A bullet hole.

Between the eyes.

Of his dead body.

It looked like a perfectly aimed shot. From someone who had been facing him. My gaze shifted to the gun in Blaine's holster and back to the body again. Then I looked behind me, wondering if one of the agents had fired the shot as they'd come running. The only thing I saw was the trunk of the big tree. I was still trying to process it all when Blaine moved in close and pulled me into his arms.

"I am now," he whispered against my hair.

He was warm. And strong. And alive. Then, it hit me. He could have so easily died protecting me today. We both could have. In the blink of an eye, our lives could have been over. I was surrounded by people who dealt with violence and death on a regular basis, but it was so far removed from my world. I was having a hard time wrapping my head around what had happened. How I'd gotten here. Then the trembling began. Full body shakes as it all came crashing down on me.

"Shh, baby. It's okay," Blaine murmured as he moved to the picnic table and pulled me onto his lap.

I'm not sure why, but the gentleness of his voice and the soft touch of his hand as he rubbed my back was enough to send me over the edge. Huge, gulping sobs wracked my body. Blaine held me through it all, providing shelter in the storm of my meltdown. I wasn't sure how long we sat there together, but by the time I'd settled down, his shirt was drenched with my tears and I felt like I could sleep for a million years.

"Sorry." My apology was a croak, low and rough, my throat feeling swollen and sore.

"It was the adrenaline crash," Blaine explained. "It hits people in different ways."

"I thought she might need this." I heard Brody's voice as an open bottle of water appeared in my line of sight, the side of my face still resting against Blaine's chest.

"Thanks," I whispered, grabbing the bottle and quickly gulping the cool liquid down. It felt like heaven, soothing my scratchy throat.

"Steele is doing her best to hold Phillips back, but he wants us in the van and he wants it now."

I groaned at the thought of having to deal with the man after everything we'd gone through. "What could he possibly want so badly?"

"He needs to debrief us, wrap everything up in a perfect little bow so he has what he needs if this goes to court," Blaine explained. "But you've done enough for today and he can damn well wait to talk to you until you're ready for his questions."

"No," I protested. "I don't want to wait. I just want to get it over with."

Blaine tilted my chin with his fingertip until I was looking into his eyes. "Are you sure you're up for it? If not, I'll tell him to go fuck himself."

I had no doubt he'd do exactly what he said, but it would only delay the inevitable. Although I felt the furthest thing from it, I injected as much strength in my voice as I was able to gather. "Yeah, I'm ready."

Boy, did I come to regret those words. Phillips had an agent ride with us in the back of the van, someone I didn't remember meeting earlier so they weren't even a friendly face. He made it perfectly clear we weren't to speak during the drive. They didn't want us to have a chance to corroborate our stories or some garbage like that. As soon as we arrived at the Atlanta field office, they separated us for our debriefing. Only, it didn't go like I thought a debriefing would. It felt more like I was being interrogated. Hours passed and Phillips didn't relent. Gone was the man who'd tried to charm me yesterday in order to get me to cooperate with his plan. In his place was a hardened federal agent with questions.

Lots and lots of questions. The ones about what I'd seen and heard today were easy since I'd been hiding under the table when the worst had happened. Besides, they knew exactly what I'd seen and heard. They were there and they had the recording from the microphone they'd wired me with before I went into the park. It was the questions about Brody that were the hardest. I didn't want to lie, but I also didn't want to give this man anything he could use against Blaine's best friend—not after he'd risked so much to keep me safe.

It seemed Phillips wasn't satisfied with the arrest. He was pissed two of the TAG henchmen had been killed, especially since Blaine had been the one who shot them both. Although I'd figured out he'd been the one to fire at least one of the shots I'd heard, I was shocked when Phillips told me Blaine killed two people today.

Then I was pissed because Phillips tried to use my surprise against me as he pushed even harder for information about Brody. It was a mistake on his part. My anger toward him helped me to hold up during his questioning. I funneled it into a steely resolve as I carefully answered with the truth, but only the parts that didn't incriminate Brody. Luckily, I hadn't actually seen him hack into anything, so I was able to word my answers deliberately, focusing on my personal knowledge only.

By the time he was done with me, it was dark outside. Blaine was nowhere in sight and I didn't want to leave without him, so I waited. And then, I waited some more, until he finally left a room a few doors down from where I had been questioned. His face looked like it had been carved from stone. As soon as he saw me, he strode to where I was sitting and held out his hand. "Let's go."

"What about Brody? I haven't seen him yet." I didn't say it, but I was worried about him. I was willing to bet Blaine's debriefing had gone much the same as mine, and I knew he wouldn't want to leave without his best friend.

He gave a quick shake of his head. "He's still being questioned, but I'm not letting you stay here a moment longer than necessary."

I wanted to protest, but he didn't give me a chance. He practically dragged me from my seat and marched me to the elevator. "But—"

His index finger covered my lips, stopping the flow of words while we waited for the doors to open. "Not here."

The ride downstairs was silent. Blaine's hand was wrapped tightly around mine, the only sign of how difficult this must have been for him. The night sky was pitch black through the windows lining the front of the building. I had no idea whether we'd be able to find a cab, but I remained quiet as we walked toward the exit. There was an urgency to Blaine and I didn't want to slow him down.

Finally, we were through the doors and on the sidewalk, but Blaine didn't slow down. He headed to the left, toward a black limousine sitting at the curb about thirty feet down the road near the closest intersection. As we approached, the back door opened and Blaine helped me inside, quickly following behind me. There was one occupant already inside—a familiar face from countless news reports and because he resembled his brother. Damian Slater had come to town.

"How bad is it?" he asked.

"It's a clusterfuck," Blaine growled. "Phillips is a dick. He's in a position of power and wants Brody's head on a platter."

"We'll just see whose head ends up on a platter once everything is said and done." Damian might not have been a former Navy SEAL like Blaine and Brody, but I got the impression he was just as dangerous.

I shifted in my seat, unintentionally drawing both their gazes my way. "Sorry," I mumbled.

"I'm the one who needs to apologize for being rude, Ms. Sinclair." Damian's reply was smooth, the formidable man from a moment ago replaced by the suave playboy the media portrayed him to be. "From

243

what I've heard, you've had quite the day already. Please allow me to drop the two of you off at the hotel so you can get some rest."

The car hadn't moved away from the curb, and I glanced out the window toward the building. "What about Brody?"

"Our team of lawyers is headed upstairs," he explained. "They'll have him out before I make it back here to pick him up."

"Are you sure you don't want to wait for him?" The question was for both of them, but I turned in my seat to face Blaine. "I feel like we're abandoning him."

"If there was any doubt in my mind about him walking out those doors tonight, we'd still be up there," he assured me. "We're not leaving him behind. Damian has this covered, and there's a lot they need to discuss sooner rather than later."

"I'm okay with waiting."

"As much as I appreciate it, we're going," he insisted.

"You've got to be at the end of your rope and it's my responsibility to make sure you have what you need. I'm going to take care of you and trust Damian to take care of his brother. He's earned it."

Damian looked surprised by Blaine's admission. I didn't understand it after hearing everything he'd done for him when Blaine had been injured. It seemed kind of obvious that Damian had more than proven himself.

Exhaustion hit me, and arguing any further about heading back to the hotel seemed ridiculous. "Okay."

I listened as Blaine told Damian the events of the last week. I was struggling to stay awake, my eyes continuing to drift shut while they were talking. It didn't take long before I gave up the battle and leaned my head on Blaine's shoulder. Darkness claimed me instantly. I slept deeply, not waking when the limousine arrived at the hotel. It wasn't until Blaine placed me gently on the bed that my eyes slid open again.

I watched silently as he removed my shoes and socks. Raised my hips so he could pull my pants down my legs. Held my arms up when he lifted my shirt over my head. And stared while he swiftly removed his clothes until he was standing in front of me in nothing but a pair of black cotton boxers.

It felt like weeks since we'd last been alone together, though it had only been this morning. At the thought of what could have happened today, the need I always seemed to feel for him quickly shot past the point of being unbearable. With a boldness I'd never shown before, I hooked a finger into his waistband and yanked him toward me. His eyes tracked my every movement as I shoved him onto his back before stroking my hand along his lower abdomen and slowly sliding it down the front of his boxers.

His hands flexed at his sides and his jaw clenched when I wrapped my hand around his hardened length. "You want to be the one in charge tonight?"

Teasing him with a light stroke, I couldn't resist lapping up the drop of pre-come on his tip before answering. "We both know who's really in charge here."

"Enough teasing," he growled. "If you want to be the one on top, you better get moving. I need to fuck. Now."

There was a desperation in his tone I'd never heard before. I swiftly pulled his boxers off and ripped my panties down my legs before I straddled him. Fingers wrapped around his cock, I dragged it through the dampness between my thighs. Moaning deeply, I guided him to my entrance and sank down slowly, inch by inch, until he filled me. His head fell back and a low growl escaped as his hips surged off the bed, sending his cock deeper. My fingers clenched against his shoulders while I struggled to hold myself still, determined to savor the feeling.

Blaine wasn't having any of that, though. His hips rolled beneath me as his hands grasped my ass in a firm, possessive hold. "You better start moving, sweetheart. Or else I'm going to flip you over and fuck you hard and deep."

"Am I supposed to take that as a threat?" I moaned, bringing my feet up and bracing them on either side of his hips. I rose up until only the tip of his cock remained inside me and then came down hard, bucking my hips. I repeated the movement over and over again, until I was bouncing wildly on his lap.

"You like taking my cock hard and fast, don't you, sweetheart?" He fisted my hair in his hand and dragged me forward to take my mouth in a deep kiss, forcing my mouth wide and driving his tongue inside. Lost in his kiss, my rhythm slowed even as my pussy began to flutter around him. By the time he tore his mouth from mine, we were both gasping for air.

"Yes," I hissed, gasping when he tilted his hips. The new angle had my body tensing. I writhed above him, each slide of his cock bringing me closer to release.

"Tell me," he ordered, hands gripping my hips and holding me in place. "I need to hear the words."

"Please," I begged, trying to wriggle out of his grasp and move so I could come. "I'm so close."

"I'll get you there, but not until you tell me what I want to hear."

"I need you, Blaine."

"That's good enough. For now," he growled. Then he lifted me off him, flipped me onto my back, and drove back in.

"Please. Please. Please," I chanted.

"Wrap your legs around me," he ordered, surging hard and deep as he jackhammered in and out of me.

"Deeper," I groaned, digging my feet into his ass. My orgasm was building—a huge one—my entire body tensing as it got closer.

He gripped my hips and started to lift me up as he thrust down. This wasn't lovemaking. It wasn't even sex. It was fucking. Pure and simple. And I liked it. No, I loved it. We'd come so close to death and each thrust of his cock made me feel alive.

"Come for me, dammit," he growled.

"So close," I panted.

"Now," he groaned into my ear. Then he bit the lobe and licked down my neck. When his teeth scraped against my pulse point, it was enough. I went flying and took him right along with me, shouting out his own release.

When my shudders ended, I rolled to my side and tucked my body along his. The nerves from this morning. The adrenaline rush from the park. The crash from my meltdown. The hours spent being questioned.

The strength of my release. It all crashed down on me, leaving me with two choices: slide into the oblivion sleep offered or break down for real this time. I chose oblivion.

****

When I woke up the next morning, Blaine was sleeping soundly beside me. His personality was magnetic when he was awake—making him impossible to ignore. He looked softer as he slept, but it didn't lessen his pull. It was incredibly difficult to let him be and roll out of bed, but I knew he needed the rest. He'd been so focused on keeping me safe, he'd barely slept all week. Resisting the urge to cuddle close, I quietly slid out of bed and crept from the room. There was plenty for me to do while he slept.

After making myself a cup of coffee, I powered up my laptop and checked to see if there were any stories in the media about our shootout in the park. I expected to find vague articles with few accurate details, but it looked like Phillips had been a busy bee last night. The first article I clicked on had facts that only could have come from his office. It described the brilliant sting operation he'd led which resulted in the capture of the mastermind behind a dangerous arms dealing operation. The writer in me was curious about what would happen next with the case, but the woman in me hoped they would be able to agree to a plea agreement. I wanted to put the whole experience behind me and move forward.

Reading the glowing account of Phillips' heroics made me want to puke, but I was relieved to see he corrected the mistaken reports of my death. Before he let me go last night, he had promised to speak with the local police. I hadn't expected him to take this extra step on my behalf, but it would be a huge help. Now I had something to share on my social media pages to help explain what happened. Since the story was stranger than fiction, the article would give my posts credibility.

The ringing of my cell phone startled me. I grabbed it quickly to accept the call so Blaine didn't hear it. *Crap! My parents must have made it back into port early. There went my plan to call them before they had a chance to listen to any of their messages.*

"I'm okay," I answered.

"Oh, thank God," my mom cried. "We had a message waiting for us from an Atlanta police officer. Of course, I assumed the worst and thought something must be wrong with you. Your dad tried to calm me down. When it didn't work, he dialed your number and handed me the phone."

"Can you put me on speakerphone? I have a lot to tell you both." When I heard my dad's voice, I started to tell them about everything that had happened since I got home from the cabin. It took forever, which wasn't a surprise since there was a lot to discuss. Plus, my mom kept interrupting me with questions. My dad remained strangely silent until the end, when he got to the heart of the matter.

"I hear something in your voice when you talk about this Blaine West guy—something more than gratitude

249

for keeping you safe. Have you developed feelings for him?"

"I have." My admission was softly spoken. I was afraid they wouldn't approve of a relationship with Blaine after the way we met.

"Serious feelings?" he asked. My dad had never been the kind of man to let me hide from my fears.

"I think I might love him."

"Oh, my sweet baby girl," my mom sighed.

"Sometimes love hits you like a bolt of lightning. It sure did for me when I met your mom. But you've just gone through an unusual experience, one putting you in a vulnerable position. Promise me you'll be careful and not do anything rash. If what the two of you have is real, then I expect to meet him when we make it back home."

"I hope it is, but I'll keep what you said in mind," I agreed. With all the emotional talk out of the way, he shifted the conversation to lighter subjects, telling me about how they'd spent the last week at sea.

By the time I got off the phone and climbed back into bed with Blaine, I felt distanced from the events of the day before. I was better prepared to turn it all around in my head. Just yesterday, Blaine had fought for me. Killed for me. If I'd had any doubts about being his before now, they would all be wiped away in the aftermath of the violence from last night. If the old saying was true, by saving my life, Blaine was now responsible for me forever.

Forever.

It was a strange word to use considering we'd only known each other six days—not even a full week—yet here I was, head over heels for this guy.

"I know you're awake, baby." I wished I was better at faking sleep or he wasn't quite so observant. Anything to let me feel his arms wrapped around me for even five more minutes before I had to face reality. Sadly, Blaine was who he was and I was who I was—which meant there was no fooling him. "If you're worried about Brody, don't be. He called after you fell asleep. Damian was right. The lawyers were able to secure his release without too many problems. They're up in the penthouse suite. Damian likes to travel in style."

"I figured he was okay based on the article Phillips managed to get onto all the media outlets this morning. He spinned it so he came out like a superhero, of course. One part was weird, though. He actually credited Brody as a valuable asset to solving the case. Just Brody. Neither of us."

Blaine's chuckle rasped over my skin. "I'm sure it's something the lawyers forced him to do. There's no way he did it voluntarily since I'm sure it killed him to share the limelight with Brody in any way."

"Well, at least he told the world I'm really alive. It made it easier when I called the police back this morning. Plus, my parents were relieved to hear the whole mess was getting cleared up with the help of the FBI. It also helped with my fans. I was able to share the story on my social media accounts since I highly doubt anyone would have believed it otherwise." I pushed up and turned in his arms, sighing at how haggard he looked. His hair was spiked up in places, his cheeks covered in stubble that went well past a five o'clock shadow. Yet, he never looked better.

"I know you slept in, but you still look like you haven't gotten more than a few hours. Maybe you should try to get some more sleep."

"Nope. We need to talk." His voice was firm as he said the four words nobody in a relationship ever wanted to hear.

"About what?" My voice was tremulous, uncertain. No doubt due to the flutter of fear his words evoked.

"You and me."

And there it was—confirmation. This was definitely going to be a talk I didn't want to have. Not now and probably not ever. Pushing farther away from him, I settled myself on my pillows, curling my arms around myself in a protective gesture. I nodded my head, trying to evoke a sense of calm while I mentally prepared myself for the worst.

"I want you to think about coming to Vegas with me."

I blinked slowly, trying to process his words, wondering if I was still asleep.

"For a visit?"

"If that's what it takes to get you to come out, then yeah. We can call it a visit."

"I don't understand," I whispered.

His jaw clenched, his gaze determined as he looked at me. "I want you in my life, Delia."

"You do?"

"Of course I do," he confirmed.

The breath I'd been holding whooshed out of me. "Don't you think it's too soon to know? We've known each other for less than a week."

"It might not have been a long time, but we've been together almost non-stop since day one," he argued. "If we'd met each other under normal circumstances and started dating, it would have taken at least six months for us to spend this much time together."

He made an excellent point. I'd probably spent more time with Blaine than I had my last boyfriend. And we'd already been to hell and back. Who was I to argue with him about wanting me in his life? It was foolish of me to disagree when I wanted the same—badly. I snuggled closer to him and gave him the answer I should have said right away. "Okay."

EPILOGUE

Blaine

Six months later

Delia's first trip to Vegas was put on hold for a different journey, one we took together to my hometown for Serena's funeral. Her mom wanted her in their family plot, down the street from the church we'd both attended growing up. I hadn't been able to save Serena from her fate, but I refused to let her make the final trek home by herself. Delia had every reason to be angry for the trouble Serena pulled her into, but she wasn't willing to let me go through this alone.

It was the first time I'd brought a woman home to meet my mom and I did it while saying my final farewell to the first girl I'd ever cared about. It wasn't exactly the way I'd planned for it to go, but Delia found a way to make everything better. As my mom struggled with the loss of the girl she'd known for years, Delia nurtured her through her grief. When Serena's mom crumbled at the idea of writing an obituary for her daughter, Delia stepped in, helping to find the right words to poignantly describe her life. While I grieved for my childhood sweetheart, she offered her support and sympathy. Delia's quiet grace made a trying time easier for everyone she met.

Our relationship quickly fell into a rhythm after that, one dictated by the distance between us—and she was on her way back to me this very moment. It was the sixth time in as many months Delia had been out to Vegas for a visit. She flew out to me and spent four or five days in town, where we were together nonstop Friday night through Monday morning—mostly in bed. When I had to go to work on Monday morning, she either spent her next couple days getting some writing done or exploring the sights. The nights were all mine, though, and she never failed to make it back to my place before I did, proving she didn't want to waste a single second of our time together.

A couple weekends after she was back in Atlanta, I'd fly out to spend a couple days at her place. Same pattern, different location—except I took a red eye flight home Sunday night so I could make it to work on Monday morning. The time always went by too quickly before I found myself back in Vegas.

This trip was going to be different, though. I'd given Delia as much time as I was willing to give. I was all out of patience. She wasn't getting back on the plane this time. The time we spent apart felt like a sin. Our relationship might have developed quickly and under unusual circumstances, but it was harder to survive the weeks I spent without her than it was to get through hell week. I didn't care if I had to tie her to my bed until she agreed to stay, it was time for her to stop playing around and move in with me.

By no stretch of the imagination did I consider myself a romantic man, but I'd done what I could to set the stage for tonight. The Italian restaurant attached to the casino would be catering dinner, and I'd ordered all her favorites. When Brody told Damian my plans, he'd sent someone from the hotel staff to set the table with linen, candles, and fancy ass plates. I bought flowers and had them waiting for her in a vase on the coffee table. Hell, I'd even sprinkled rose petals on the bed. Since she'd written a hero who did the same thing in one of her books, I figured it was something she'd appreciate.

It wasn't the first time I'd borrowed an idea from one of her books—the last time involving chocolate sauce and messy sheets. I didn't feel quite as pussy whipped reenacting that scene, but I was only going to propose once in my life and I was damned sure going to make it good.

I was doing one last sweep of the apartment, making sure everything was exactly the way I wanted it, when I heard her walk in the door. She liked to get in before I got home from work so she could get settled and I hadn't wanted to tip her off that anything was different. I sent a car for her like I always did, but this time, I was ready and waiting for her.

"Surprise," I said softly as I watched her drop her bag on the ground. She was staring at the flowers on the table and I started to wonder if I'd gone a little overboard with the size of the bouquet.

As soon as she heard my voice, her eyes jerked to me and then she was running across the room to throw herself into my arms. "I missed you so much."

"Missed you, too," I whispered, my arms tightening around her as I lifted her off the ground. It felt good to have her close again. Damn good.

I captured her mouth with mine, savoring her taste, our tongues tangling together. She whimpered a low sound deep in her throat. Gathering her hair in a fist, I tilted her head and took the kiss deeper. By the time I moved away from her lips, we were both flushed with desire and breathing hard.

"I hate missing you. It's getting harder to leave each time even though I know I'll see you again," she admitted.

It wasn't the way I'd planned to do this, but she just gave me the perfect opportunity. I wasn't one to squander an opening like this. Now was as good a time as after dinner. I hoped.

"Then don't leave again."

Her eyes looked surprised when she looked up at me. "You want me to move in with you?"

"No, I want you to marry me," I corrected. I pulled the ring from my pocket and got down on one knee in front of her. "Marry me."

Tears streamed down her cheeks as she smiled down at me. "Are you asking me to marry you or telling me I'm going to?"

"Telling." She raised her eyebrow in response. "Fine, I'm asking. Delia Ann Sinclair, will you be my wife?"

"It will be my pleasure and my honor."

"Thank fuck," I sighed, sliding the ring onto her finger.

"It's about time," she whispered. "I'm crazy in love with you, but I was starting to wonder how long I was going to have to wait until you asked."

"Crazy in love is the perfect way to describe my feelings for you, too." I didn't know how it was possible, but her face became more radiant at my words. "If I'd known, I would have asked before I ever left you in Atlanta the first time. And now that I know I wasted six months, I'm not waiting for fucking ever while you plan the perfect wedding."

"Even if it's what I really want?"

"Fuck," I sighed, knowing I'd wait if that were what it took to make her happy. But I'd damn well do it with her in bed next to me the whole time. Then I heard her giggle and caught the gleam in her eye. "Are you messing with me?"

"It's Vegas, baby!" she cried.

"This weekend."

"Next weekend," she conceded. "I'm fine with a Vegas wedding, but I still want the perfect dress, flowers, and cake. My parents will also need enough time to fly in. Mila, too."

It was a hell of a lot sooner than I thought she'd make me wait. I could last two weeks until I made her my wife. If I had to. "I'll handle the rest, and I promise it won't be some tacky wedding chapel in town." I waved my hand toward the table in the kitchen. "Damian arranged this in less than an hour after he found out I was going to propose tonight. I've seen some of the weddings they've had at his hotel. He'll be able to help me set up something amazing for you."

"And what will I be doing while you're handling all the wedding details?" Her voice held a hint of sass, a knowing tell she was thinking about starting an argument over this. If she was going to get mad, I figured I might as well make it worthwhile.

"You're going to start out by celebrating our engagement this weekend. Then, when you get back to your house this week, you're going to pack it all up and ship it out here so you can move in with me before we get married. Somewhere in there, you can figure out the dress, cake, and flowers. I'm sure Mila will help."

"Cyan, too," she mumbled. "I think I'll have two bridesmaids at this wedding you're planning for me. So you better make sure you have two groomsmen. It's the least you can do if I'm going to be a crazy person up until our wedding. And we're going to look for houses as soon as we get back from the honeymoon. Which better last for at least two weeks. Or else."

"Consider it done." A two-week-long honeymoon might give us time to see something besides our hotel room. "Brody already told me he's my best man. I'll ask Damian to be a groomsman."

"I'm pairing Brody up with Cyan." Her eyes lit with a knowing look. She was up to something and it wasn't hard to figure out she was hoping to do a little match-making between the two.

Brody had been acting strange lately. I'd been preoccupied, trying to juggle work and my long distance relationship with Delia. But now that I had her exactly where I wanted, I needed to pay closer attention to what was going on with him. After our honeymoon, of course. Until then, I had a wedding to plan for my woman and a ton of work to wrap up before we left. It didn't leave me with much of a choice but to trust my best friend to have his own shit covered for the next few weeks.

259

WHAT'S NEXT IN THE CRISIS SERIES?

SECURITY CRISIS

Yes, I am going to write books for Brody and Damian. Originally, I had planned on Identity Crisis being a standalone, but these things have a way of changing once I get to know some of the supporting characters better.

Security Crisis will be Brody's story. If you don't want to miss out on news about the release of his book, please make sure you've joined my email newsletter.

Sign up online at: http://eepurl.com/Ly1Tn

OTHER BOOKS BY THIS AUTHOR

BLYTHE COLLEGE SERIES

Push the Envelope

Hit the Wall

Summer Nights (novella duo)

Outside the Box

Winter Wedding (novella)

BACHELORETTE PARTY SERIES

Sucked Into Love

BLACK RIVER PACK SERIES

Crying Wolf

Shoot For the Moon

Thrown To the Wolves

McMAHON CLAN SERIES

Bear the Consequences

261

COMING SOON FROM CP SMITH

FRAMED

Six hundred minutes. That's all it took for trouble to find ex-SEAL Kade Kingston his first day home. He'd managed to survive covert operations in the hostile mountains of Afghanistan, only to be brought down by a baseball bat. If he had the first five hundred minutes back, he would have only had one drink before insisting Stan Sutton tell him what the hell was going on. As it stood now, he and Sutton were both dead in the water—literally and figuratively. Six hundred minutes. That's all it took for Kade Kingston to walk back into hell in his own backyard, losing everything in the process, including his freedom.

Inmate dog trainer, Harley Dash, knew Kade briefly as a teenager and was convinced of his innocence. Wanting to help the brooding ex-SEAL, she took it upon herself to force Kade into the Inmate Dog Training Program. While Kade was confined, Harley and her father, along with two sexy SEALs, looked for evidence that would set him free.

Sutton's murder was just the tip of the iceberg in a case of corruption and murder, one that will send Kade and Harley into the Florida Everglades with a killer in hot pursuit.

Will they survive the mosquitoes and alligators of the Everglades, or will the Dread Pirate Roberts exact his revenge?

ACKNOWLEDGMENTS

My boys – Thank you for not complaining too much about the piles of laundry & carry-out meals while I was writing. Yes, I know... yet again. I love you!

Mom – Thank you for always supporting me and inspiring me to live my dream.

Yolanda – Thanks for being a great friend. Even though we live states away from each other, your continued support means the world to me.

Monica – Thank you for putting your attention to detail to good use for me. This story wouldn't be nearly as good without your help.

Panty dropping Book Blog – Thanks for your help getting the word out about my books. Heather has been great and you all have done an amazing job pimping me! The bloggers that work with you have been so generous with their time and efforts on my behalf.

Tijan – I owe the title to you! Thanks.

Readers/Bloggers – Thank you from the bottom of my heart for taking a chance on me. I would not be living my dream right now if it weren't for all of you.

ABOUT THE AUTHOR

I absolutely adore reading—always have and always will. When I was growing up, my friends used to tease me when I would trail after them, trying to read and walk at the same time. If I have downtime, odds are you will find me reading or writing.

I am the mother of two wonderful sons who have inspired me to chase my dream of being an author. I want them to learn from me that you can live your dream as long as you are willing to work for it.

When I told my mom that my New Year's resolution was to self-publish a book in 2013, she pretty much told me, "About time!"

Connect with me online!
FACEBOOK:
http://www.facebook.com/rochellepaigeauthor
TWITTER:
@rochellepaige1
GOODREADS:
https://www.goodreads.com/author/show/7328358.Rochelle_Paige
WEBSITE:
http://www.rochellepaige.com

28654376R00147

Made in the USA
Columbia, SC
16 October 2018